GHOST STORY

GHOST STORY

Jamal spoke out loud as he typed. "Hello, computer. My name is Jamal. Ready for one dynamite dude?"

Suddenly an eerie yellow sparkle sped around the room right in front of his eyes. It zoomed to the letters on the keyboard and then right into the computer itself!

Terrified, Jamal jumped up, knocking his chair onto the floor. He held his breath. The computer screen suddenly went blank. Then new words glowed into focus.

HELP HELP HELP HELP! WHERE ARE THE CHILDREN? ARE THEY ALL RIGHT?

JOIN THE TEAM

Do you watch GHOSTWRITER on PBS? Then you know that when you read and write to solve a mystery or unravel a puzzle, you're using the same smarts and skills the Ghostwriter team uses.

We hope you'll join the team and read along to help solve the mysterious and puzzling goings-on in these GHOSTWRITER books!

GHOST STORY

A novelization by N. H. Kleinbaum
Based on a teleplay by Kermit Frazier

A CHILDREN'S TELEVISION WORKSHOP BOOK

BANTAM BOOKS
NEW YORK • TORONTO • LONDON • SYDNEY • AUCKLAND

READ THIS REBUS!

A Bantam Book / December 1994

Ghostwriter, **Ghost**_{writer} and ● are
trademarks of Children's Television Workshop.
All rights reserved. Used under authorization.

Art direction by Mary Sarah Quinn
Cover design by Susan Herr

ISBN 0-553-48272-6

Published simultaneously in the United States and Canada

Bantam Books are published by Bantam Books, a division of Bantam
Doubleday Dell Publishing Group, Inc. Its trademark, consisting of the
words "Bantam Books" and the portrayal of a rooster, is registered in the
U.S. Patent and Trademark Office and in other countries. Marca Regis-
trada. Bantam Books, 1540 Broadway, New York, New York 10036.

PRINTED IN THE UNITED STATES OF AMERICA

OPM 0 9 8 7 6 5 4 3 2 1

CHAPTER 1

Twelve-year-old Jamal Jenkins climbed over a pile of boxes, pushing his way toward the corner of the crowded, dusty basement.

He picked up the cover of a tattered box. Inside was an old baseball cap, one of his forgotten favorites.

"Hey, look what I found!" Jamal cried. He waved the navy and white cap at his father, Reggie, who was kneeling in another cluttered corner of the basement.

"That trunk's got to be in here somewhere," his father grumbled.

"Think it's going to be big enough to hold Danitra's stuff, Dad?" Jamal asked.

"It'd better be or I'm going to have to rent a U-Haul to

get your sister off to college," his father said. "Hey, wait, I think I see it, Jamal!"

Reggie pulled a yellowed old sheet off the trunk, which had been wedged onto the bottom row of some crowded shelves.

"Looks really old, Dad," Jamal said. "Do you think it's sturdy enough?"

"It belonged to your great-grandpa Ezra. They don't make 'em like this anymore. Help me get it out."

Reggie tugged at the trunk as Jamal pushed on the other side. They didn't see a tattered, brown leather book fall from a high shelf onto the floor. As the book's yellowed pages fell open, a bright royal-blue glow pulsed for a moment and then zoomed across the basement.

As they climbed the creaky basement stairs, their backs were turned on the eerie blue light that was zooming crazily around the basement. It bolted frantically into corners and under boxes, bounced off walls, and crawled through crevices.

Reggie glanced back at Jamal, who was struggling under the weight of the trunk. "You okay?" he asked.

"One minute, Dad, my hands are slipping," Jamal said. He readjusted his grip, unaware that the strange blue glow had jumped onto his back and was silently bouncing from letter to letter on his T-shirt.

"Okay, I got it," Jamal said.

"My goodness, do you remember that old thing?" Grandma CeCe said as the two emerged into the living room. "My, my, but that does bring back memories."

Reggie smiled, watching his mother fuss over the trunk. "Lots of good memories, huh, Mama?" he said.

"Lord, yes!" she chuckled. "All kinds!" She turned to Jamal. "Could you do me a favor, Jamal? I'm making my famous caramel cake as a surprise for Danitra but I need some more milk. Would you run over to the store for me?"

"Sure, Grandma," Jamal said. "One carton or two?"

"One's just fine. Now you be careful walking near the park, you hear? It's starting to get dark."

Jamal raced over to the small market near the park. He bought the milk and started home.

It was pitch-dark as he walked quickly along the street, humming to himself and practicing his karate kicks. Suddenly he heard moaning sounds coming from the park.

Jamal stopped near the entrance to the park. He squinted, looking toward the sounds. In the dark, four ghostly creatures were flitting around a huge red metal sculpture. They wore strange masks that covered their whole heads and seemed to have faces in front and in back. Jamal moved closer, trying to get a better look. He watched them jump and dance like frightened insects, moving their arms wildly as they howled and moaned. Their faces, with huge bulging eyes, twisted mouths, and scarred skin, glowed from the light of flashlights they held under their chins.

Suddenly, one of the creatures turned and looked directly at Jamal. The creature stood still for a second, then darted into the blackness of the park.

Jamal gulped in terror. His feet were frozen to the ground. But then his curiosity won out over his fear. He raced into the park toward the statue, trying to get a closer look at the creatures, but it was too late. They were gone.

Jamal stopped and looked around. His heart was pounding and he was breathing heavily. He glanced around the park, and then hugged the milk carton to his chest as he turned toward home.

Jamal started walking briskly but then slowed to a stop. He stared back into the silent, shadowy park. He was sure he had seen something, somebody. But had they seen him? He shivered and clutched the milk carton tighter. Jamal hurried home and sprinted up the steps and into the living room.

"Here's the milk, Grandma," he said, handing it to her.

"Thanks, honey. Are you all right? You look like you've seen a ghost or something," Grandma CeCe said.

"Nah, I'm fine," he said, but his heart was still thumping hard.

A minute later Danitra's voice rang out from a corner of the living room. "I can't get my trunk closed!"

"Try jumping up and down on it four or five times," her father answered.

"Daaadddd!" she whined. "I *need* you!"

Danitra's voice softened as she tried another tactic. "Jamal, would you come here a minute? I need you to plop yourself on this and help me get it shut."

"You're going to need more than Dad or me to help close that," Jamal said as he eyed the overstuffed chest. "Did you pack up your whole room?"

Danitra smirked. "Not everything. In fact, since you are

my favorite brother, I left my computer in your room and you can use it—"

"I'm your *only* brother," Jamal interrupted.

"Well, anyway," she said. "You can use it. Just don't break it, you hear?" She raced up the stairs.

Grandma CeCe came in from the kitchen. "Thanks for going to the store, Jamal. Leave it to your old grandma to run out of milk right in the middle of making my special caramel cake."

"Do I get some or is it all for Danitra?" Jamal asked hopefully.

"It's a going-away-to-college present for her, sweetheart. Now you know that. But I'll make one for you soon. Okay?"

Jamal sighed and headed for the stairs. This off-to-college business was too much. Danitra this, Danitra that! Suddenly he remembered the computer. He dashed into his room and closed the door behind him, shutting out the noise from the rest of the house. He looked around his room.

He'd carefully chosen his favorite sports posters and tacked them up where he could see them while he did his homework. Family pictures hung on one wall. His book-case was crammed full of his favorite books and magazines. A dartboard hung on the back of the door.

Then Jamal saw it. The computer sat in the middle of his desk. Danitra had even set it up for him. Jamal felt a little pang of guilt. Danitra wasn't such a bad sister, he thought.

Jamal threw his jacket on the bed, next to the orange T-shirt he'd changed out of after he helped his father move the trunk. He sat in front of the computer, flicked on the screen, and began typing.

He didn't notice the bright glow, now a neon orange, flowing out from under the T-shirt on his bed. It raced like a meteor around the room and then jumped from letter to letter on the posters, calendar, and fliers on the walls.

Jamal spoke out loud as he typed. "Hello, computer. My name is Jamal. Ready for one dynamite dude?"

Suddenly an eerie sparkle, now yellow, sped around the room right in front of his eyes. It zoomed to the letters on the keyboard and then right into the computer itself!

Terrified, Jamal jumped up, knocking his chair onto the floor. He held his breath. The computer screen suddenly went blank. Then new words glowed into focus.

HELP HELP HELP HELP! WHERE ARE THE CHILDREN? ARE THEY ALL RIGHT?

Jamal stared, and swallowed hard.

"'Help help help help! Where are the children? Are they all right?'" he read aloud. "Children? What children?" Jamal said to the computer screen. "What are you talking about? Who *are* you?"

There was no response. He looked around at the back of the computer and then at the screen again.

The message was still there.

Jamal rushed to the door and yanked it open.

"Danitra!" he shouted.

"What?" she called from her room next door.

"Come here for a minute, and hurry!" he said.

"I'm busy," she answered.

"Just come in here, okay? It's important."

Jamal quickly righted his desk chair and then stood by the door waiting for Danitra. He was ready to run if necessary, but still transfixed by the strange message on the screen.

"What is it?" Danitra asked impatiently when she finally came in.

Jamal pointed to the computer. "That. What's that?"

Danitra rolled her eyes. "It's a computer, Jamal. You play games on it, write letters, even send messages to your friends! Everyone is using them these days. It's the one I'm letting you have, remember?"

"Read what's on the screen," he said nervously.

Danitra looked at the computer and shook her head. "There's nothing on the screen, Jamal. It's blank. You have to turn it on."

Jamal's heart pounded loudly in his chest. "What do you mean there's nothing on the screen?" He turned to look at the screen, where the message still glowed.

"It says, 'Help help help help! Where are the children? Are they all right?'" Jamal almost shouted. "So what is it? Some kind of secret computer game or program or something?"

Danitra shook her head. "Look Jamal, if you can't use the thing, I'll be happy to—"

"I'm not saying that," he said quickly.

"Then I suggest you chill out, be a wee bit more appreciative, or at least halfway sane. Maybe you've been reading too many science fiction books or something," she said as she stalked from the room.

Jamal walked back to the computer. He looked at the screen.

"This has got to be one of her tricks," he said with a sigh.

He sat down before the screen and tried to get rid of the message. He hit the Escape button on the keyboard but nothing happened.

"Oh, man," Jamal said, slamming his hand on the desk. "What *is* this?"

He frantically followed the computer cord to the wall outlet and yanked out the plug.

The message dimmed and disappeared from the screen.

"Got ya!" He sighed, relieved to see the screen go blank. He sank back into the chair.

"Jamal?" his sister called from next door.

"What?"

"Will you come here for a minute, please?"

"Sisters," he muttered, but he got up quickly, glad to be leaving his room for a while.

As Jamal shut the door behind him, the pulsating glow reappeared. It flowed silently out of the computer and into his backpack.

CHAPTER 2

Gray, dreary clouds hung over the skyline in the Fort Greene section of Brooklyn as ten-year-old Gaby Fernandez walked slowly to school, singing out loud.

"Sunshine! Oh where are you sunshine . . . ," she belted out, off-key. Up ahead, her thirteen-year-old brother, Alex, turned around and winced.

"Fairness in weather, fairness in weather!" Gaby shouted, her arms outstretched. "I protest this miserable weather!"

Alex Fernandez walked quickly, shaking his head in annoyance. He gulped the last of his orange juice and tossed the container into a garbage can. "*Swish!* Basket!" he congratulated himself.

"Did you know that St. Petersburg, Florida, once had seven hundred and sixty-eight days of sunshine in a row? That's over two whole years of sunshiny days!" she reported to her brother.

"Tell that to your teacher, why don't you," he called back. "And hurry up, will you?"

Gaby walked faster, her ponytail swishing as she sped up.

Alex stopped and turned to Gaby. "Look, I don't know about the Washington Elementary School, but at mine, kids have to arrive sometime *before* the school day ends."

Gaby stuck out her tongue. Alex ignored his pesky sister and moved on, picking up his pace. Gaby stopped and knelt.

"Wait a minute, Alex," she called. "My shoe's untied."

But Alex didn't hear her and kept walking. He turned the corner and was gone. Gaby started to tie her shoelace. Suddenly a shadow loomed over her.

"Gee, big brother," she said sarcastically, without looking up. "Thanks a lot for waiting for me. I—"

Suddenly a big hand grabbed her backpack.

"Hey," Gaby cried. "Wait a—"

She jumped up in time to see a big kid wearing a mask with two faces—one in front of his head and one in back—running away with her backpack.

Gaby ran to the corner. "Alex!" she called. Tears of anger and fear streamed down her cheeks.

"Darn!" She sobbed loudly and raced ahead, trying to catch up to her brother.

At the same time, Jamal Jenkins headed out the door for Zora Neale Hurston Middle School with his backpack slung over his shoulder. He hadn't been able to forget what he'd seen the night before. Without thinking twice, he headed to the park where he had seen the strange creatures. As Jamal stared at the huge red metal sculpture, he tried to remember the details of the ghoulish masks and the weird sounds the dancers had made.

"Nothing," he said out loud. "Not a sign of it! Could I have been dreaming?" He shifted the heavy backpack to his other shoulder and started off toward school. As he turned to walk, an eerie light pulsated slightly in his backpack, but Jamal didn't know it was there. He stopped and looked back at the sculpture as his mind flashed to the scene of the wild, spooky creatures he'd seen.

Jamal didn't notice twelve-year-old Lenni Frazier heading in his direction. Lenni had her nose buried in her songbook as she walked. She bumped right into Jamal.

Startled, she dropped the songbook.

"Gee, I'm sorry," Lenni quickly said, her bright brown eyes apologetic. She flung her backpack to the ground and bent to pick up her book just as Jamal reached to get it for her.

As they knelt together the mysterious glow, now a bright shade of pink, flowed from Jamal's backpack into Lenni's.

They started talking at the same time.

"Listen, I should have been watching where I was going. I'm sorry," Lenni said, a friendly smile lighting up her face.

"Nah, I should have been watching where I was standing," Jamal said. He smiled back.

"Lenni, right?" Jamal asked.

"Yeah, Lenni Frazier. You're Jamal. I've seen you at school."

They grabbed their backpacks during the awkward silence that followed. Lenni held up her songbook.

"I'm working on a new song," she said. "I guess my mind was on my music, that's why I walked into you."

"Oh, really? Yeah, I remember. You sang in the talent show."

Lenni nodded and her face broke into a proud grin. She'd been singing and writing songs ever since she could remember.

"You were pretty good," Jamal said.

"Thanks," Lenni said. "Well . . . see ya, Jamal."

"Yeah . . . see ya!"

Lenni walked to a bench and sat down. She opened her songbook and began writing busily.

Jamal turned his attention back to the red sculpture. He walked up to it and began to circle it, inspecting the ground. He looked around. There was no one nearby. He looked back down. Staring up at him was a big neon-green button. He picked it up and peered at it.

"THABTO," he read out loud. "What could that be?" He turned the button over and saw a sticker with a figure of a cat wearing a party hat. Jamal stuck the button in his pocket and continued to circle the sculpture. On the other side he saw a folded light-blue piece of paper lying on the grass.

"What's this?" he said, picking it up. He opened the paper and stared at the block letters on it:

ZRRGVAT SEVQNL FRCGRZORE GJRYSGU
GUR SVANY FRPERG PRERZBAL
ORTVAF ERAEBP LINA QENL

Oh, man, what is this? he thought. *More weirdness!*

He stuffed the paper in his pocket with the button and headed off to school.

Still sitting on the park bench, Lenni had lost track of time as she worked on finishing her rap song.

Suddenly the bright pink glow that had been hidden in Lenni's backpack swirled onto the words in her songbook. Lenni dropped the book and gasped, "What . . . what's that?"

She watched wide-eyed as the letters jumbled, rearranging themselves on the page of her book.

WHERE ARE YOU, DYNAMITE DUDE JAMAL? read the new words.

Lenni threw the book to the ground and backed away. She picked up a large stick that was lying on the grass and poked the songbook. As quickly as it had come, the glow disappeared and the words Lenni had written returned. Lenni sighed with relief and poked the book again for good measure. Just then the eerie glow reappeared.

The letters on the page jumbled around again. This time the message read: LENNI FIGHTS FOR WHAT'S RIGHT.

"Wow!" she shouted. She grabbed her backpack and spun on her heel, ready to run down the street. Something made Lenni stop and turn back. She walked hesitantly toward her songbook, which was lying open, its pages blowing in the slight breeze that had come up. There was no sign of the eerie pink glow.

Lenni scooped the book up like a hot potato and shoved it into her backpack. She raced down the street to school. Huffing and puffing, she joined the throng of Hurston students just as the first bell rang.

Lenni ran through the hallway, nearly knocking over two girls.

Down the hallway, Jamal stopped at his locker. He noticed a folded slip of paper shoved through one of the locker slits. He unfolded the paper, and read:

Near the park
After dark
You were there
So BEWARE!!!

The note was signed THABTO. Jamal fished the THABTO button he had found in the park out of his pocket. The button went flying onto the floor as Lenni rushed up, knocking into Jamal.

"All right, Jamal, how'd you do it?" she asked.

Jamal bent to pick up the button, looking at Lenni curiously.

"Do what?"

"Was it some kind of magic trick?" Lenni asked.

"What?"

"Was it something from science lab I missed?" she continued.

"What are you talking about?" Jamal said.

Lenni took out her songbook and opened it to the page she had written in the park. She held it up to Jamal's startled face.

"Change the letters around. I dare you!" she ordered.

"Look," Jamal said, pushing the book away. "I don't know what you're talking about. And this is the second time today you sneaked up on me and nearly knocked me down!"

He pulled out the folded paper and held it in front of her face.

"You're probably sneaking notes into my locker, too, huh?"

"What?" Lenni cried, grabbing the note. She scanned it quickly.

"I didn't write this," she said, looking up at Jamal. "And who is THABTO?"

Jamal shrugged. "I don't know. I *was* near the park after dark last night, though. I saw these strange faces. And I heard these creepy sounds. This morning I went back to look around. That's when I saw you. I found this button there," he said, handing the button to Lenni.

"And this strange message, too," Jamal said, handing Lenni the paper with the garbled words in block letters.

"Scary stuff," she said, quickly handing them back to Jamal.

"Tell me about it," he said. "I can't figure it out and I can't stop thinking about it."

"Maybe you'd better throw them away," she said anxiously.

"Uh-uh," Jamal said. He smiled devilishly. "This is just weird enough to be really interesting. A real mystery or something!"

He held out the threatening note from his locker and they both looked at it again.

While they read the note the eerie glow reappeared, sweeping across the words and jumbling them up as it bounced in a green swirl from letter to letter.

"Jamal!" Lenni whispered, reaching over and clutching his hand. She squeezed it hard.

"I know! M-M-Me, too!" he stuttered.

They watched as the glow left the note and swept across the hallway, landing on a huge bulletin board covered with posters, fliers, and signs about the school lunch program.

The glow rearranged the letters. The bulletin board read:

CAREFUL AFTER DARK, MY CHILDREN.

Jamal and Lenni looked around to see if there was any reaction in the crowded hallway.

"Nobody else sees that!" Lenni said.

"Shhh! People will think we're nuts if we say anything," Jamal whispered. "Just act natural." They looked at the bulletin board again. The letters were back in their original positions.

"That's what happened in my songbook in the park!" Lenni said.

"Well, I didn't do it," Jamal assured her.

"I know that now. But your name was mentioned when the letters moved around so I thought it was you!" Lenni quickly filled Jamal in on the way the letters in her songbook had spelled out two different messages. "Who *did* do it? Who's doing this to us?" she asked.

Jamal shook his head. "I don't know. But it is kind of exciting, isn't it?" He grabbed a piece of paper and quickly scribbled down his address.

"Look, can you come over to my house after school? I think I've got something really weird to show you. Maybe it's related."

"Okay," Lenni said, sticking the address in her pocket. "I'll be there."

CHAPTER 3

Gaby Fernandez stood in the middle of her parents' small grocery store, her eyes bright with excitement and fright as she told them how her backpack had been stolen.

"He just swooped down like this giant eagle and grabbed it up, while I was bending down to tie my shoe!" She knelt down, demonstrating how she'd been taken by surprise.

Eduardo and Estela Fernandez watched their daughter with fear and anger on their faces.

"I even chased after him," Gaby boasted. "Might have caught him, too, if my shoelace hadn't been halfway untied."

Mrs. Fernandez hugged Gaby tightly. "It's a good thing you didn't catch him. You could have been hurt."

Mr. Fernandez stood silently. "Did you tell the teacher?" he finally asked.

"Yes, Papa. A couple of other kids have also had their backpacks stolen. There must be some kind of gang or something," Gaby said.

Mr. Fernandez turned to Alex, speaking rapidly in Spanish. "*¿Y tú, dónde estabas mientras tu hermana perseguía al ladrón?*" he asked. "And where were you while your sister was chasing a thief?"

"Sorry, Papa," Alex said apologetically. "I'd already turned the corner when it happened. I didn't see or hear anything."

"But you're supposed to walk Gabriella to school!" his father said sternly.

Alex lowered his head. "I know, but she walks so slowly."

"It wasn't Alex's fault, Papa," Gaby said, trying to save her brother from punishment.

Mr. Fernandez looked from Gaby to Alex. "From now on I want you to stay with Gabriella all the way to school. *Comprendes?*" he said sternly.

"*Sí*, Papa," Alex said. "I'll walk Gaby all the way to school from now on."

Mr. Fernandez threw up his hands. "A backpack stolen. Schoolbooks, supplies, lunch money! It all costs!" he muttered as he went behind the deli counter.

He turned to his daughter. "At least my Gabriella wasn't hurt this time," he said. "Both of you be careful and look out for each other from now on."

"*Sí*, Papa," Alex and Gaby both said. They picked up their things and headed toward their apartment behind the bodega.

"At least he didn't punish us," Alex said. "Thanks for sticking up for me, Gaby."

"You owe me one," she said. They walked into the room they shared. A sheet had been hung down the middle to make a partition. Gaby flopped onto her bed.

"I think this really is some kind of gang thing," she said.

"Pretty low thing to do," Alex said. "Picking on little kids. But who would do this, and why?"

"Alex," Mrs. Fernandez said, poking her head into the doorway, "I have to take care of these receipts. Will you watch the register for a little while?"

"*Sí*, Mama," he said, heading out of the bedroom and back to the store.

Alex was sitting on a stool behind the counter absorbed in a detective story when the bells jangled above the bodega's front door. Lenni hurried into the store. She headed over to the vegetables, eyed them carefully, and scooped up a lettuce, four tomatoes, two peppers, and a cucumber.

She walked to the counter and cleared her throat to get Alex's attention. He slowly lowered the book, his eyes still dreamy and far away.

"Hi, Lenni," Alex said.

"*Hola*, Alex," she answered. She placed the vegetables on the counter.

"Another detective novel?" she asked.

Alex began ringing up Lenni's items on the register. "Yeah, I'm halfway through it and I think I've already figured out who committed the crime."

"Then why bother finishing it?" Lenni asked.

Alex smiled. "Just to prove I'm right! Anything else?" he asked, pointing to the food.

"Nope, that's it."

"Three sixty-five," he said as he put the veggies into Lenni's woven bag.

Lenni handed Alex the money just as the sound of a wailing saxophone and the flourish of a drumroll came loudly through the ceiling.

Alex looked up at the sound. "Your dad and his band have been going at it all afternoon," he said, pointing to the ceiling.

Lenni smiled apologetically as she scooped up the bag of groceries. "They're rehearsing for a big job at the Red Snapper Club this weekend. I'll go and check on the music and see that they give you a break. Bye!" Lenni said.

Lenni trotted out of the bodega and up the narrow staircase to the sprawling loft apartment she shared with her father.

She opened the door quietly. Inside the high-ceilinged, oversized apartment, Max and his jazz quartet wailed their music at fever pitch.

"Take five!" Max said when the group reached the end of the piece.

"Hey, Bips," he called to Lenni.

"Hi, Dad."

"Thanks for getting the groceries, honey," he said, kissing her on the forehead.

"Sure. No problem," Lenni said. "Listen, can I go over to Jamal Jenkins' house for a while?"

"Jamal Jenkins?" Max asked. "Do I know him?"

"Sort of. You met him at the sixth-grade dance you helped chaperone last year," she said.

Max laughed. "I met a million kids at that dance, Bips."

"Please, Dad! He's helping me on a project and he lives right down the street. Two blocks away."

"Well . . ." Max hesitated. "Okay. But don't be too late."

"Thanks," Lenni said, grabbing her songbook and heading for the door.

"Tonight's my special spaghetti sauce," Max shouted after her.

"I wouldn't miss it for anything!" she promised. "Bye, Dad."

As she closed the door, she heard him say, "Let's pick it up again." The jazz group swung loudly to life.

So much for the Fernandezes' music break! she said to herself.

Lenni raced down the stairs and ran the two blocks to Jamal's house. She wondered what he could possibly have to show her.

Jamal and his family were in their living room getting ready to see his sister off to college.

Danitra was in a panic, nervously stuffing clothes, shoes, and trinkets into the last bag to be put in the car.

"All right now, have we *finally* got everything?" her father asked, groaning as he lifted the bag.

"Yes, Dad."

"Good, because one more bag and there won't be any room in the car for any of *us*!" he said, as everyone laughed.

"All right," Danitra's mother, Doris, said proudly. "Let's get this young woman off to the University of Pennsylvania!"

"You take care of yourself, scholarship girl, you hear?" Danitra's grandmother said.

"What's that?" Reggie Jenkins asked suspiciously as Grandma CeCe handed Danitra a paper bag.

"My leek-and-potato soup, three-bean salad, cake . . . you know, *food*!" Grandma CeCe said.

"Mama, she's not going to some desert island. She's going to Philadelphia," said Reggie.

"So? Everybody knows college food's not home cooking!"

Danitra patted the bag. "Thanks, Grandma. I love you."

She turned to Jamal, who sat awkwardly on the arm of an overstuffed chair, not quite believing that his big sister was really leaving.

"Aren't you going to say good-bye?" Danitra asked.

Jamal hung back. "Bye," he said flatly.

Danitra walked over to Jamal and hugged him tightly. He put his arms around her shoulders, hugging her back. He blinked hard, not wanting to cry in front of the whole family.

"I'm going to miss you, Jammy Jam."

"I'm going to miss you, too," he said, stepping back quickly and adding, "I *guess.*"

Danitra threw a pillow at Jamal. "You!" she laughed.

"All right, let's hit the road!" their father said.

"We'll see you Sunday evening," Doris Jenkins said to Grandma CeCe and Jamal.

"Okay, we'll be fine," Grandma CeCe said.

"Jamal," Mr. Jenkins said, "you mind your grandmother, you hear?"

"Yes, sir."

They waved good-bye and closed the door. Two minutes later, the doorbell rang. "Now what did she forget?" Grandma CeCe said. "I didn't think she'd left anything here."

"I'll get it," Jamal said, hurrying to the door. He opened the door and saw Lenni holding her songbook.

"Hi," he said.

Lenni walked into the living room and Jamal introduced her to his grandmother.

"Well," Jamal said. "We're going to go upstairs and work on the computer for a while."

"Okay, sugar, have fun," his grandmother said as they headed up the stairs.

CHAPTER 4

"This is my room. The computer's over there," Jamal said. "That's where I read 'Help help help help! Where are the children? Are the children all right?' on the screen. And when I showed it to my sister, she didn't see a thing!"

The kids walked cautiously toward the computer. Jamal plugged it in and turned it on. Lenni stood anxiously behind him waiting for something to happen.

Jamal shook his head. "Nothing!" he groaned.

"Maybe this'll help," Lenni said, placing her songbook next to the computer. "This is where the words of my song were changed around by whatever this computer thing is!"

They watched silently.

"Come on, come on," Jamal said impatiently. "Where are you? *Who* are you?"

"This really is weird," Lenni said. She looked around while they waited. "Nice room," she told Jamal.

"Thanks," Jamal said. "Hey, I know what we can do. Let's try and figure out that weird note. It's been driving me crazy!"

He unfolded the blue paper. "Does this make any sense to you?" he asked, handing it to Lenni.

ZRRGVAT SEVQNL FRCGRZORE GJRYSGU
GUR SVANY FRPERG PRERZBAL
ORTVAF ERAEBP LINA QENL

She looked at it and shook her head. "Looks like some foreign language . . . like Greek or Russian or something," she said.

"Which I don't read or speak," Jamal sighed. "Do you?"

"Nope," Lenni said. "How about trying a mirror?"

Jamal held the paper up to the mirror over his dresser.

"Forget it," Lenni said. "It makes no more sense than the first way. It's *worse*."

Jamal stared intently at the message and suddenly laughed out loud.

"What's so funny?" Lenni asked.

"You know why we can't read this?" he asked, not waiting for an answer. "Because it's probably written in some secret code."

Lenni's face brightened. "Hey, yeah. And I know just the person who can help us out, too!"

"Who?" Jamal asked.

"Alex Fernandez. You know him? His parents own the bodega on Prospect. My dad and I live in the apartment upstairs. He's always reading mysteries and usually he can solve them before he finishes the book!"

"Yeah," Jamal said, recalling the tall, dark-haired boy in his school. "I sometimes see him hanging around in the video arcade."

"Right," Lenni said, getting up to leave. "Listen, I've got to go. My dad's making dinner and I said I'd be home. But Alex is good at figuring stuff out. You should show this to him."

"Good idea. Could you call him before you go?"

While they looked for Alex's number, Grandma CeCe was downstairs getting ready to go to the market.

She walked to an end table and picked up the short grocery list. She didn't notice a pulsating blue glow flashing on her list of *milk, cheese, potatoes, cornflakes.*

The glow shined brightest on *cornflakes* but faded as Grandma CeCe picked it up and slipped it into her coat pocket.

"Jamal," she called from the foot of the stairs. "I'm running to the store. I'll be back in a few minutes."

"Okay, Grandma," he called back.

Lenni bent over the telephone book looking for Alex's number.

Suddenly the computer screen caught Jamal's eye.

"Lenni, look!" he gasped as she turned from the telephone book. She stared at the screen in disbelief.

WHAT IN THE WORLD ARE CORNFLAKES? the screen read.

Jamal raced to the computer and stared at the words.

Lenni's jaw dropped open as she eyed the computer screen.

"What'll we do?" she asked.

"Talk to it or something!"

The two kids stared at the words on the screen. Both began talking nonstop to the computer.

"Who are you? Where do you come from?" Lenni asked.

"Where have you been? Don't you know what cornflakes are?" Jamal demanded.

Jamal held his breath as he looked from the screen to Lenni. She looked as if she had seen a ghost. The pair peered at the message on the screen for what seemed like a long time.

"Wait!" Lenni shrieked, grabbing Jamal's arm. "It's writing again!"

WHAT IN THE WORLD ARE CORNFLAKES? WHY DO YOU NOT ANSWER ME? the screen read.

"'Why do you not answer me?'" Jamal read aloud, scratching his head. What was the computer trying to tell him? How could he talk to it?

"We *are* answering you," Lenni said to the screen.

"Do you want us to speak louder?" Jamal shouted.

ANSWER ME ANSWER ME ANSWER ME ANSWER ME ANSWER ME ANSWER ME ANSWER ME, the screen responded.

The kids stared back dumbfounded.

"What do we do now?" Lenni said.

"I don't know!" Jamal answered.

They jumped at the knock on the door.

"Jamal?" Grandma CeCe called from outside the door. "I'm back already!"

"Okay, Grandma," Jamal answered without opening it.

"Is everything all right in there?"

Jamal looked at Lenni and the computer screen.

"Uh, yeah . . . sure," he said.

"I brought you and Lenni a snack," Grandma CeCe called from the hallway.

Jamal opened the door and Grandma CeCe walked in carrying a tray of cookies and two glasses of juice.

"Thanks, Grandma," Jamal said, smiling weakly.

"Yes, thank you very much, Mrs. Jenkins," Lenni added. She picked up a glass of juice and took a gulp.

"What was all that shouting about?" Grandma CeCe asked suspiciously.

"Oh, that, yeah. That's just some crazy computer game," Jamal said, laughing.

"Really! Can I see it? I want to learn about computers," Grandma CeCe said. "Computers are everywhere! In the supermarket, at the bank . . ."

She walked to the computer screen and stood in front of it.

"Well, where is it? It's blank. I don't see any game here."

Jamal and Lenni looked at each other and back at the screen, where the message ANSWER ME ANSWER ME ANSWER ME ANSWER ME ANSWER ME ANSWER ME ANSWER ME still stood out boldly.

"We got bored," Jamal said quickly, taking a cookie from the tray.

"It was getting too complicated," Lenni added. She bit into a cookie. "These are delicious, Mrs. Jenkins. Did you bake them yourself? I love homemade chocolate chips."

"Oh, yes, I love to bake," Grandma CeCe said. "I'm disappointed I couldn't learn your game. Next time you play let me know, okay?" She left the room.

"She didn't see it!" Jamal whispered after his grandmother had closed the door behind her.

Lenni munched on the cookie. "How come we're the only ones?"

Lenni sat down on the bed and stared at the screen. She thought about the message on the computer and how they had tried to answer. There had to be a way to communicate with this voice inside the computer. *What could it be?* she thought.

"Maybe it can't hear us," Lenni said finally.

"That's it!" Jamal cried. "It's writing to us. Maybe we should write back."

Jamal sat at the computer and cleared the screen.

"Who are you?" he typed.

I DO NOT REMEMBER, came the response.

Lenni leapfrogged off the bed and stood next to Jamal at the computer. "All right!" she said excitedly.

"We did it!" Jamal beamed. "It can't hear but it can read and write."

"Where did you come from?" Jamal typed onto the screen.

I DO NOT KNOW was the answer.

"Are you a person or an alien?" Lenni said to the screen. She stared, waiting for an answer.

There was no response.

"We've got to write," Jamal said. "Otherwise it can't understand us."

"Can I write some?" Lenni asked, feeling frightened and excited by this strange turn of events.

"Sure." Jamal got up and Lenni slid into the chair.

"Are you a person or an alien?" she typed.

A PERSON, the screen said. OR AT LEAST I WAS.

"A he or a she?" Lenni typed.

A HE.

Lenni shook her head and looked at Jamal. "In a computer?" she asked.

She changed places with Jamal. "Why do you live in my computer?" he typed.

WHAT IS A COMPUTER? the screen responded.

Jamal and Lenni sighed. "Oh, no!" they said in unison.

I FEEL LOST, the screen said.

Lenni looked at the screen. This voice in the computer had feelings and emotions. She looked at the computer and imagined she saw a person.

"Let's tell him where he is," Lenni suggested to Jamal.

Jamal moved over to let Lenni type again.

"You are in Jamal's room. Brooklyn. New York. The United States," Lenni typed.

She turned to Jamal. "Is that enough?"

"Earth. The Universe," he said, and Lenni quickly typed those words.

OH was the response on the screen.

Jamal looked at the screen. "Do you still feel lost?" he asked.

"Type it," Lenni reminded him. The two quickly switched places.

"Do you still feel lost?" Jamal typed.

The "Oh" response on the screen faded out.

"Wait," Jamal called.

"What's wrong?" Lenni asked.

The screen came back to life. I FEEL SAD AND LONELY, it read for a moment, then faded away again.

"Sad?" Lenni said in a surprised voice. "He's fading away! No, don't go now! We just got started!"

Jamal stared at the blank screen. "He's gone."

"Come back," he typed. There was no response.

"Oh, no," Lenni moaned. This was more than either of them had expected. Lenni looked at the computer screen and felt as if someone were dying.

"We've got to get him back. But how?" Lenni said. She took a deep breath. "Well, let's think logically. What do we know about him?"

"We know he's scared and lonely," Jamal said. "And he's worried about children. He's also worried about us and said not to go out at night. Let's tell him we are his friends and we care about him. Maybe he won't feel scared."

The screen remained blank.

"Let's tell him he isn't alone," Jamal said. "Tell him we'll be his friends. That might make him stay."

"Quick, let's do it. It may be too late," Lenni cried.

"We'll be your friends," Jamal typed on the screen. "Then you won't be lonely."

"Quick! What else can we say?" Jamal asked Lenni. She stared at the screen, her mind racing. Time was running out! Suddenly she smiled.

"I bet this will do it," she said. She reached over Jamal's shoulder and typed: "We'll write to you."

After a moment, the screen came to life.

THANK YOU! I'LL WRITE TO YOU, TOO.

Jamal and Lenni jumped in the air and gave each other a high five.

"Yes!" Jamal shouted, raising his fist in triumph.

"He's back!" Lenni cried, hugging the computer screen. "We did it. What do we call him?"

Jamal shook his head. "I don't know. He says he's a person . . . or at least he used to be."

Lenni turned to Jamal, her brown eyes wide with disbelief. "You mean he's . . . a ghost?"

Jamal shrugged. "I don't know. Maybe we can call him . . . ah . . ."

Lenni laughed. "Ghostperson?"

"Ghostperson! Like, 'Yo, Ghostperson?'" Jamal said.

"How about Ghostwriter?" Lenni said.

"Now you're talking. He's a ghost and he writes to us. Ghostwriter," Jamal said and nodded, liking the way the name sounded.

"Let's see what he thinks," Lenni suggested.

She sat in front of the computer. "Can we call you Ghostwriter?" she typed.

There was no response.

The two kids looked at each other worriedly and then back at the screen. Suddenly the screen lit up as words began to appear letter by letter.

I LIKE THAT NAME, Ghostwriter responded.

Lenni and Jamal shook hands happily. They grinned widely at each other and Jamal leaned over and thumped the computer affectionately.

"Good job, Lenni," Jamal said.

"All right!" she agreed. "Now I've got to get home for dinner or my dad will have a fit."

"Bye, Ghostwriter," Lenni typed into the computer. "Talk to you soon!"

CHAPTER 5

Jamal dropped a large stack of hardcover books onto his desk with a thump. He grabbed a piece of paper and wrote on it, "Here are some of my dad's books about New York, Ghostwriter."

In seconds Ghostwriter's glow swirled out of the computer screen and over Jamal's note. Then it pulsed around and through the books.

Jamal picked up his homework and tried to concentrate on math, his toughest subject. His attention kept drifting to Ghostwriter's glow in the books.

Meanwhile, Lenni had raced the two blocks to her apartment and up the stairs, bounding loudly into the loft.

"I'm back, Dad!" she called.

"Hey, just in time," he said. "I thought I was going to have to eat alone. Here, taste."

He held out a spoonful of sauce to Lenni and she tasted it.

"Mmmmm . . . makes me want to eat forever!" she said.

Lenni threw her jacket on the couch and grabbed plates and silverware to set the table.

"So, you made a new friend today," Max said when he and Lenni sat down to eat.

"Two."

"There was somebody else at Jamal's?" he asked.

Lenni realized she had let out too much information. She wasn't ready to tell her father about Ghostwriter.

"Uh, yeah, his grandma," she fudged. She looked down at her spaghetti.

"You hung out with his grandmother?" Max asked, raising one eyebrow.

"Yeah, kinda, sorta. She brought us snacks when we were playing computer games. She's real nice. Kinda cool!" Lenni smiled, and dug into her spaghetti. *That's true,* she thought.

While the Fraziers enjoyed their dinner, Jamal was back at the computer screen, playing a sports game. He was so into the game, he didn't see Ghostwriter zoom off the stack of books and land on the THABTO button on Jamal's desk. The letters glowed as Ghostwriter read them. Suddenly

Ghostwriter zipped out the bedroom window and into the street.

Ghostwriter landed on an identical THABTO button that was pinned to the jacket of a big kid standing in the park. The big kid lurked behind a tree watching two little boys on skateboards. He scouted the park, noticing two other little boys sitting on a bench. One had left his backpack next to him while he focused on a handheld video game.

Slowly the big kid pulled a double-faced mask from his pocket and lowered it over his head. He gave a final tug to the mask, then burst out from behind the tree and rushed up to the bench. He snatched the backpack and ran into the bushes.

Still entranced by the game on his computer screen, Jamal never noticed that Ghostwriter had left and returned.

"Ha ha! Creamed you!" Jamal laughed out loud.

Suddenly the screen went blank.

"Hey, what happened?" Jamal said, looking at the screen.

THABTO AMERICAN FLYER SPORT, the screen read.

"Ghostwriter!" Jamal cried. "What's he writing?"

Jamal looked down at the THABTO button on his desk and back at the coded message on the screen.

"THABTO?" he said out loud.

Jamal began typing. "Ghostwriter, are you . . ." Suddenly he stopped typing as his mind flashed back to the park and the scene of the scary creatures wildly dancing behind the red sculpture.

Jamal gasped and pushed away from the computer.

"Oh no!" he said. "Is Ghostwriter THABTO?"

Jamal took a deep breath and moved back to the computer.

"Ghostwriter," he wrote, screwing up all his courage. "Are you THABTO?"

WHAT IS A THABTO? Ghostwriter wrote.

"Something bad, I think," Jamal said out loud as he typed the words onto the computer screen.

I AM NOT BAD!!! Ghostwriter responded immediately.

Jamal thought about the words on the screen and realized that Ghostwriter was hurt.

"I know you're not, Ghostwriter. I'm sorry," he typed. "Where did you read about THABTO?"

ON ANOTHER THABTO, Ghostwriter responded.

How did Ghostwriter find another THABTO button? wondered Jamal.

"Can you travel?" he typed to Ghostwriter.

YES! FROM ONE WORD TO ANOTHER, Ghostwriter responded.

Jamal sat back and stared at the screen. "From one word to another," he mused. "Ah-ha!"

"Jamal," his grandmother called. "Dinner!"

"Coming!" he said. He turned off the computer.

"Talk to you later, Ghostwriter," he said and headed down the stairs.

Saturday morning dawned bright, sunny, and warm. Jamal stretched in his bed, happy not to have to race to school.

He'd had a restless night thinking about the last two days.

Was Ghostwriter for real, or was it just a dream? He looked around the room. On his desk sat a stack of books about New York City and next to his computer was the neon-green THABTO button.

"Where could Ghostwriter have seen that word?" he wondered, pulling on his favorite faded, baggy jeans and a T-shirt.

"Grandma, can I go over to the video arcade?" Jamal asked he walked into the kitchen.

"Did you have your breakfast?" she asked.

"I'll have some cereal," Jamal said, pouring a bowl of puffs and drowning them in milk.

"Where'd you say you wanted to go, sugar?" Grandma CeCe asked.

"The video arcade. It's Saturday so there'll be a lot of kids there," Jamal said between gulps of cereal.

"Okay," she said. "But don't stay all day."

"Thanks, Grandma, I won't," he said, heading out the door. He stopped and turned back.

"Grandma?"

"Yes, sugar?"

"Do you believe in ghosts?"

She chuckled. "I hope you're not leaving me here with that question hanging in the air."

Jamal smiled, waiting for Grandma CeCe to continue.

"No," she said thoughtfully, "I don't. Not unless they're the good friendly kind that live in memories. Why do you ask? What've you been seeing lately?"

"Nothing," Jamal said, shaking his head. "Just thinking. Bye."

"Bye, yourself," Grandma CeCe said as Jamal closed the door behind him.

CHAPTER 6

Bright lights and loud pings, pongs, and gongs greeted Jamal as he walked into the packed video arcade. Groups of kids hung around more than a dozen video-game machines, cheering and hissing as they fed quarters into the slots and challenged each other to contests.

Jamal spotted Alex Fernandez at a machine near the back. Alex punched the knobs furiously as he reached the highest level of the game.

Behind him on the wall of the arcade hung a huge sign: DOUBLE DEFENDERS TOURNAMENT, SATURDAY SEPTEMBER 13TH, 12 NOON.

Jamal walked up to the machine where Alex was playing. He noticed a detective novel stuffed into Alex's back pocket.

"Hi! Alex, right?" Jamal asked as he watched Alex play. Alex turned to Jamal.

"Oh, yeah. Hi, Jamal." He smiled.

The machine went quiet and Alex fumbled in his pockets. "Oh, man," he said, slamming his hand against the machine. "I can't be out of quarters. I just made top ten!"

Jamal poked into his pockets. "Sorry, Alex. I've just got two dimes," he said.

Alex shrugged. "Thanks anyway. I probably spent enough money on these games today anyhow," he said.

He and Jamal turned toward a noisy crowd of kids gathered around a Double Defenders machine with a hot game in progress.

Four kids—three boys and a girl—were furiously playing the Double Defenders video game as a gang of onlookers cheered.

"Wow! They're really going at it!" Jamal said, watching the serious players.

"Yeah," Alex said, pointing to the sign. "Big tournament next week."

"Hey!" Jamal said, getting excited. "Wouldn't it be really cool if the Double Defenders were real and could actually play in the tournament?"

"Aw, man! That'd be awesome!" Alex agreed. "All the superheroes competing against each other to find out who's best. I bet the X-MEN wouldn't need any quarters to play!"

"Neither would the Turbo Heads," Jamal added. "I wonder who would win if the Double Defenders went up against the Turbo Heads?"

42

"Aw, man, are you kidding me? The Turbo Heads would blast the Double Defenders out of the galaxy!" Alex said.

"I don't know, man," Jamal said, shaking his head. "Those Double Defenders are *baaaadddd!* They have two heads and can see behind themselves and everything!"

"Yeah, but the Turbo Heads are supercharged! They've got engines where their brains used to be, and lasers in their eye sockets."

"Yeah." Jamal relented. "I guess you're right."

Alex took the detective novel out of his back pocket and placed it on the machine, digging one last time for quarters.

"That's it. I'm busted. No more quarters," he said.

Jamal picked up the book and read the title, *The Sleuths.* "Aren't they a singing group?" he asked.

"No, they're kid detectives," Alex said. Jamal handed the book back to Alex.

"Speaking of detectives," Jamal said as they started to walk out of the arcade, "Lenni Frazier tells me that you're good at solving puzzles and mysteries and stuff."

"Well, not really good," Alex said. "I'm *great* at it!"

Jamal chuckled. "All right, Your Greatness," he said as he took the paper with the coded message out of his pocket, "why don't you take a look at this message?"

Jamal handed the light-blue paper to Alex.

ZRRGVAT SEVQNL FRCGRZORE GJRYSGU
GUR SVANY FRPERG PRERZBAL
ORTVAF ERAEBP LINA QENL

"Lenni and I think it's some kind of code. What do you think?"

"Yeah, it's a code, all right. Pretty tough one."

Jamal handed the THABTO button to Alex. "I found the note yesterday morning in the park. This button was there, too. I also saw these creepy-looking creatures moaning like out of a horror movie or something . . ."

Alex looked closely at the THABTO button.

"And yesterday at school," Jamal said, "I found this note in my locker warning me to be careful. It was signed 'THABTO.'"

"Hmmm," Alex said. "Now this is what I call a mystery! What do you say we take these codes to the World-Renowned Fernandez Laboratory for further analysis?"

"I'm with you, my man," Jamal said.

A short time later, the boys walked into the bodega, which was busy with Saturday-morning shoppers. Jamal followed Alex to the apartment at the back of the store.

"I have to share this room with my little sister, Gaby," Alex explained, pointing to the sheet that divided the room. "She needs her privacy," he added, rolling his eyes.

"I have a sister, too," Jamal said. The two nodded sadly to each other and then broke into grins.

"Okay, now, the codes," Alex said, getting down to business. "You know codes have been around forever. Once we find out what kind of code this is, we can start to decode it."

"How?" Jamal asked, impressed.

"There are two different kinds of codes," Alex

explained. "One that replaces each letter with a different letter or number. Like this . . ."

Alex opened his desk drawer and pulled out a small chart, showing it to Jamal. It showed the letters of the alphabet with the numbers one to twenty-six underneath, so that there was a number for each letter.

A	B	C	D	E	F	G	H	I	J	K	L	M
1	2	3	4	5	6	7	8	9	10	11	12	13

N	O	P	Q	R	S	T	U	V	W	X	Y	Z
14	15	16	17	18	19	20	21	22	23	24	25	26

"Take the word *eggs*," Alex suggested, writing it on the paper. He pointed to the chart.

"You can see in this code *E* is *5* and *G* is *7*—"

"Oh, I get it," Jamal interrupted. "So a different number stands for each letter."

"Right . . . so if you want to write *eggs* in this code you write *5 7 7* . . ."

"That's for *egg*," Jamal said, "and the *S* is *19*."

Alex wrote *19* under the letter *S*.

"Right," he continued. "There is also another code where you substitute letters for letters."

"I see," Jamal said. "So maybe *A* could be *E*."

Alex nodded. "Right. Then there's a whole different code where you scramble all the letters up in a word. Like this . . ."

Underneath *eggs* he wrote *gesg*.

"Then you get scrambled eggs!" Alex said, as both boys fell into fits of laughter.

"Hey, that's pretty cool," Jamal said. "Let's try that on our coded message."

They took out the folded paper again:

ZRRGVAT SEVQNL FRCGRZORE GJRYSGU
GUR SVANY FRPERG PRERZBAL
ORTVAF ERAEBP LINA QENL

"Look, I see one already," Jamal said excitedly. He circled *GUR*. "See this? This could be *RUG*," he said.

Alex studied the code. "Great."

Jamal circled the word *PRERZBAL*. "I think I see *ZEBRA* here," he said. "See, there's a *Z . . . E . . . B . . . R . . . A*."

"Yeah, but there's a *P, R,* and *L* left over," Alex said, shaking his head.

Jamal frowned. "Oh, yeah."

Alex studied the message. "This can't be a scrambled code!" he said.

"Why not?" Jamal asked.

"Look at the last word," Alex explained, circling the *QENL*. "No matter how you change these letters around, you can't make that a word. There's a *Q* but there's no *U*. And *Q* and *U* go together in any English word."

Jamal scratched his chin. "Yeah, I see. That must mean that this code—"

"Replaces letters with different letters!" Alex concluded excitedly.

"We're gonna crack this code, I can feel it in my bones," Jamal said.

The bedroom door flew open as Alex's sister, Gaby, rushed in breathlessly.

"Alex, come quick. I need your help. I think I know where my stolen backpack might be!"

"Where?" he asked.

"In this junkyard where my friend Katya found her backpack. She said they only took her money. So maybe there's something left in mine, too. My trivia book, or my pencil case, my notebook, something—"

"Hold it, hold it. Slow down, all right?" Alex said.

"Why?" Gaby asked impatiently. "We've got to get there before it's too late."

"The least you could do is say hi to Jamal," Alex said.

Gaby hadn't even noticed Jamal. "Oh, sorry. Hi, Jamal. I'm Gaby. You can come, too."

She stood up and turned to Alex. "Okay? Now let's go!"

She raced from the room. Alex shrugged. It was hard to ignore his sister's orders, even if she was younger.

"We better go with her," Alex said.

The boys followed Gaby out of the room and through the bodega to the junkyard several blocks away. It was on the edge of the city, a dirty pile of old cars, discarded appliances, broken bicycles, and abandoned baby carriages. The kids pushed through some rusting metal gates and walked down a path between high heaps of junk.

"Four more kids in my class alone have had their backpacks stolen since last week," Gaby told Jamal, looking all around as she talked. "The whole school's starting to get scared. And it's bigger kids who are doing the stealing, too. Like middle school, or something."

"Man, what a drag," Jamal said.

"But you don't ever see their faces because they wear these weird-looking masks."

Jamal stopped searching and looked at Gaby.

"Weird masks?"

"Yes," Gaby continued. "These humongous, bulging eyes and snotty, twisted noses and warts and moles on every inch of their skin and—"

"All right, all right," Alex interrupted. "We get the picture. It's gross!"

Jamal's mind flashed back to the scene in the park when he had seen the strange-faced creatures behind the red sculpture. His flashback ended abruptly as he heard Gaby shouting.

"I found it!" she shrieked, pointing up to her backpack. She tried to pull it down from a tall water pipe stuck into an old toilet bowl, but couldn't reach. Jamal got it for her.

"Well?" Alex asked as Gaby started looking through the backpack.

"Yep, my lunch money's gone, all right, but everything else is here."

"Thanks, big brother," she said, standing on tiptoes to give Alex a kiss. "You, too, Jamal."

"No problem," he said.

"Well, I'll see you," Gaby said perkily as she headed toward the gates out of the junkyard.

"Hey!" Alex called. "Where are you going?"

Gaby shouted back over her shoulder, "To tell Tina Nguyen about this. She's making a video about me. I mean about the thefts."

"Papa says you have to stick with me, remember? Especially when you have your backpack," Alex said.

"But Tina lives right here on this block. Just three doors down. Don't worry. I'll be okay," she said, quickly walking through the gates.

Alex sighed, shaking his head. Jamal laughed. "Oh, boy. She's some character!"

Alex watched as Gaby trotted down the street. Jamal wandered around the yard and noticed another backpack hanging from another junkyard sculpture. The backpack read AMERICAN FLYER SPORT.

That sounds familiar, Jamal thought as he reached up for the backpack. Suddenly he remembered the computer screen message from Ghostwriter: "THABTO American Flyer Sport."

"Find something?" Alex asked.

"Yeah," Jamal said. "Another back . . ." He stopped in his tracks, his voice trailing off as he stared at Alex's jacket, where the embroidered name ALEX pulsated with the yellow glow of Ghostwriter.

"What's wrong?" Alex asked Jamal, seeing the strange expression on his face.

Alex followed Jamal's gaze down to the front of his own jacket. His eyes grew wide. He stumbled back and fell into a pile of garbage cans.

"What is that thing?" Alex asked, sounding really scared.

The glow zoomed off Alex's jacket and over to a wall covered with graffiti.

"You can see that?" Jamal asked in surprise.

"What do you mean? Of course I can see it! What do you think I am, blind?" Alex answered without taking his eyes off the moving light.

The now purple glow zipped and swirled across the graffiti-strewn wall. Suddenly the glow began moving the spray-painted letters around. A new message appeared on the wall: ALEX: LOVER OF MYSTERIES.

"'Alex, lover of mysteries,'" he read about himself out loud. "Oh, wow!"

Jamal and Alex stood transfixed by the glowing message.

"Jamal, what's going on?" Alex asked.

"It's Ghostwriter, man!" Jamal said. "And he's writing to you!"

CHAPTER 7

"**G**hostwriter? Are you nuts or something?" Alex said as the letters suddenly dripped away from the wall and the original graffiti came back.

"It's gone . . . oh, man, this is weird," Alex mumbled. "Stolen backpacks, aliens. What's next?"

"Calm down," Jamal said, trying to calm down himself. "He's not an alien. He's Ghostwriter."

Alex began laughing almost hysterically. "Hey, come on. Be serious. Coded messages are one thing, but *ghosts*?"

"I am serious," Jamal assured him.

"You mean to tell me that thing, those glowing letters or whatever they are, belongs to you?"

Jamal started, "No, he—"

Alex stepped back anxiously. "Then you belong to him?"

"*No,* he—" Jamal tried to explain.

"You went to another planet and back or something?" Alex said, laughing nervously.

"Just chill, okay, Alex?" Jamal said. "Besides, Lenni can see him, too."

"Lenni?" Alex looked shocked. "Who else knows?"

"I don't know," Jamal admitted. "I thought it was just the two of us until you . . ."

Alex looked all around him. "So what is he then?" he asked.

"Well . . ." Jamal hesitated. "You might not want to hear this . . ."

"What?" Alex demanded. "Tell me!"

"We think he might be a ghost," Jamal said, quickly adding, "but we're not sure."

Now Alex was curious. "So where does he live? How does he live?" he pressed. "Is he on a mission? How does he know my name? Why? . . ."

"Whoa, Alex, whoa," Jamal said. "I just saw him myself for the first time two days ago!"

"You *saw* him?" Alex asked, squinting in disbelief. "C'mon, Jamal. What is this, a joke?"

"I saw his writing, I mean," Jamal said. "Look, Alex, he's a friend. He wants to be friends with us."

"Why us?"

"We don't know. All we know is that he doesn't know

who he is or where he came from. And that somehow he's connected to words."

Alex slumped against the iron fence. *This is incredible,* he thought. He loved to read mysteries and solve the make-believe ones. But to be in the middle of a real mystery was something else.

"We also know that he can read words in one place and print them out someplace else." Jamal pointed to the words AMERICAN FLYER SPORT printed on the backpack he had found.

"He read these words yesterday and sent them to me," Jamal explained. "He also read the word THABTO in the same place. That might mean THABTO and the stolen backpacks are connected!"

Jamal and Alex looked at each other, then scouted around the junkyard cautiously, suddenly fearful that someone else might be there.

"Yeah, well, whatever we do, first we've got to return this bag to this Felix kid," Alex said, pointing to the name tag, which also had an address.

"Yeah, and we've got to tell Lenni about you and Ghostwriter!"

"Ghostwriter," Alex said, shaking his head as he and Jamal walked toward the street. "What a trip!"

After dropping the backpack at the owner's house, the boys headed over to Lenni's apartment loft.

By the time they got there, Alex was jumping with excitement.

"This Ghostwriter stuff is really cool!" he said for the

umpteenth time as he paced in the section of Lenni's loft that was set up as a living room. Big, brightly colored couches formed a comfortable U-shape, setting the area off from the kitchen.

"Imagine! An invisible, secret partner. Just think of the possibilities! Like, he can help us with schoolwork," Alex said.

"Hey, yeah," Lenni piped up. "Maybe he can read books and do book reports for me."

The excitement was contagious. "Maybe he could do math for me!" Jamal said. "I hate math tests!"

"Probably just word problems," Lenni said, and laughed.

"Yeah. Word up, right?" Jamal said. They all giggled.

"Hey, hey, listen," Alex said, drawing the trio into a huddle. "Maybe he can even give us answers on tests!"

"Hey, yo! Ghostwriter," Alex shouted fearlessly, "can you give us answers on a test?"

"He can't hear you, remember?" Jamal pointed out.

"You've got to write it down," Lenni explained.

"Ghostwriter," Alex wrote, "can you give us answers on a test?"

Ghostwriter's glow pulsated suddenly and sharply over the words in Alex's question.

As the trio watched, he pulled letters from the words and wrote below it: THAT WOULD E C EATING.

"Whoa!" Lenni said. "What's that?"

Jamal pointed to the message. "That would something something *eating*?" he read out loud.

"What's *eating* got to do with what I asked him?" Alex asked.

Jamal shrugged. "I don't know."

Lenni studied the words. "Wait a minute," she said. "You asked him if he can give you answers on a test, right?"

"Yeah," Alex said.

"And what do you call it when you give somebody answers on a test?" Lenni continued.

"Cheating," Alex said, his face turning red.

"So *eating* must be *cheating*," Lenni agreed.

"Right," Alex admitted.

"It says, 'That would be cheating.'" Lenni filled in the missing letters and the message glowed.

"Hey, cool," Jamal said.

"Well, at least he's honest," Alex noted.

"Which means he won't be reading our diaries and stuff if we don't want him to," Lenni pointed out.

Alex looked perplexed. "But why did he leave those blank spaces?"

"He took the letters from the question you asked and wrote his answer out with them," Jamal explained. "Those were the only letters he had to use."

"I guess he can only use letters that are nearby," Lenni observed.

"Except for when he's in a computer. Then he can write anything," Jamal said. He read the message and Ghost-writer's answer.

"We should let him know we're honest, too. After all, we wouldn't really ask him to cheat for us," Jamal added.

"I guess not," Alex said. He took a piece of paper and wrote "Just kidding" to Ghostwriter.

"I wonder if Ghostwriter could help us figure out who's stealing backpacks," Lenni mused.

Jamal jumped up. "That's a great idea! Sure he can. Ghostwriter wants to help us. He helped us the first time when he sent us that THABTO message."

He took the THABTO button out of his pocket and turned it over in his hand.

"I still say this button is connected to the backpack thefts," Jamal insisted.

"What about the coded message?" Lenni asked. "That might be connected, too. You did find the message and the button in the same place."

Alex nodded in agreement. "Yeah," he said. "So cracking the code has got to be our first step in getting our hands on those backpack-busting bullies."

"Let's ask Ghostwriter if he can find more THABTO buttons," Lenni suggested, as she reached for a piece of paper.

"Yeah, maybe he can even help us crack the code," Jamal suggested.

"Hey, cracking codes is *my* specialty," Alex objected.

"Then how come you haven't cracked it yet?" Jamal asked. "Besides, it's *my* code!"

"Do you have it now?" Alex asked. "It's sitting on *my* desk at home."

Jamal's usually warm brown eyes clouded with anger. "That's only because—"

"Hey, you guys! That's enough!" Lenni said. "Look, are

you going to be fighting all the time? Because if you are we can just call it quits right now, okay?"

Alex and Jamal stared at each other for a moment. Lenni's words hung in the air.

"Truce?" Alex said, putting out his hand.

"Truce," Jamal agreed, reaching out to shake.

"Okay," Lenni said. "Now I'm writing to Ghostwriter!"

"Can you help us find more THABTO buttons, Ghostwriter?" she wrote on a piece of paper.

The words jumbled in a golden glow.

I CAN TRY! Ghostwriter replied.

"All right, Ghostwriter!" Jamal smiled as the three friends shook hands together.

"Why don't we make up some kind of special Ghostwriter handshake?" Alex suggested.

Lenni shrugged. "Like what?"

"Let me see," Alex said, taking Lenni's hand. They grabbed wrists, shook hands while putting the thumb and pointer finger together, and then punched fists three times.

Alex and Jamal quickly repeated the secret shake.

"The Ghostwriter seal of approval," Alex said.

"Our secret." Lenni smiled.

"Just the three of us," Alex whispered.

"And don't forget Ghostwriter!" Jamal reminded them.

Later that night, Jamal sat before his computer screen, thinking about Ghostwriter and the new friends he had made.

"Why did you choose us?" Jamal wrote to Ghostwriter.

Instantly, the screen glowed.

SOME THINGS YOU JUST FEEL! it read.

Jamal stared at the screen as he pondered Ghostwriter's words.

"Ghostwriter is right again," Jamal said. "Some things you just feel."

Jamal Jenkins and his father wrestle with a heavy trunk, unaware that they've knocked over an old book and let Ghostwriter loose!

Lenni Frazier is so into writing a rap that she doesn't see Ghostwriter zooming into her bag.

Jamal and Lenni are stunned when Ghostwriter zooms onto a bulletin board at school and rearranges the letters to send them a scary message: CAREFUL AFTER DARK, MY CHILDREN.

Jamal introduces Lenni to Grandma CeCe without letting on that the two have met to get to the bottom of a mystery.

Jamal writes to his new friend Ghostwriter on his computer.

Alex Fernandez sees the glow of Ghostwriter for the first time—it's a huge surprise!

Tina Nguyen makes a video of Alex's little sister, Gaby, as Gaby describes how a big kid in a creepy mask stole her backpack.

When Gaby is done, Tina gives her a smile.

Alex (above) and Jamal (right) think carefully about the strategy they'll use when they call someone who might be mixed up in a backpack-stealing scheme.

Alex, Jamal, Lenni, and Gaby get a visit from Ghostwriter.

Gaby gives Lenni a happy squeeze. She's glad they're all working together to solve a mystery.

It was them! A girl who had her backpack stolen points out the culprits.

When the young thieves try to escape, they run into the police.

Jamal explains how he and his friends gathered clues to figure out the identity of the backpack thieves.

After the action dies down, Jamal sits in his bedroom and thinks about the new friends he's made, including Ghostwriter.

CHAPTER 8

"It was like being set upon by some incredibly hungry, giant green pterodactyl from prehistoric times," Gaby said. Her brown eyes open wide, she looked into the lens of Tina Nguyen's video camera, hoping to capture the terror of the moment.

"Luckily his food interests didn't include sweet, innocent girls like me," she said, laughing.

Tina made a face behind the camera and signaled to Gaby to continue.

"And then there's that junkyard where—"

"Cut!" Tina called, shutting off the camera. "I know that part already, Gaby. Thanks."

Tina set down the camera, which had WASHINGTON

ELEMENTARY SCHOOL written in bold letters on its side, and recorded the video shot in her logbook. She looked over the other notes she'd gathered and circled three important comments that were repeated by three victims.

"You know," Gaby mused, sitting on her bed as Tina jotted down more notes, "I've always wanted to be a newscaster. Do you think you might need an anchorperson for your—"

"No thanks," Tina said. "All I need are the facts. I've got the story." She smiled at Gaby, who shrugged. Gaby liked Tina. She was smart and pretty. Her dark, bright eyes and long, shiny hair always made her stand out in a crowd. But Tina didn't seem to notice it, Gaby thought, which was what made her even nicer.

The girls looked up as Alex and Jamal walked into the small room, talking nonstop.

"So I figured if we looked again at my codebooks—" Alex said. He stopped midsentence as he noticed Tina sitting on the bed.

"Oh, hi." He smiled shyly.

"This is my friend, Tina Nguyen," Gaby said, noticing her brother's particular interest. "She's a fifth-grader at my school. Also a big-time reporter for Washington School's Action News Team."

Gaby tried not to laugh as she watched Alex's face. Her big brother was standing there silently, and he was starting to blush.

Tina looked straight at Alex. "Not that big-time, really." She laughed.

"Tina, this is my brother, Alex, and his friend Jamal," Gaby said, finishing the introductions.

"Hello," Tina said.

"Hi," Jamal said.

Alex kept staring until Jamal nudged his arm. "Oh. Hi, Tina," Alex said.

"She's the one I told you about who's doing the story on the backpack thefts," Gaby explained.

"It's really terrible what's been happening," Tina said.

"I know," Alex agreed dreamily. He knew he was staring at Tina but couldn't seem to help himself. The room was silent except for a giggle Alex thought he heard coming from his dumb little sister.

"It really is terrible," Jamal agreed, breaking the silence.

"There have been fourteen victims already," Tina said. "Eight girls and six boys. The really creepy thing is that most of them said the thief was wearing a goggly-eyed mask that made him look like he had two faces!"

"I could swear that's what I saw last week in the park," Jamal whispered to Alex. "Last Thursday night."

"I'll get a notebook," Alex whispered back as the girls began packing up the camera equipment. "We have to write down everything for you know who. And so we don't forget, too!"

Tina picked up her things and headed for the door as Alex bent over his notebook. He started to write down all the things he and Jamal had learned as well as what he'd heard from Tina.

"Well, thanks for the info," Tina said.

"Wait a minute!" Gaby shouted at her brother. "What are you doing?"

"What does it look like I'm doing?" he asked.

"This is Tina's story, not yours," Gaby said angrily. "Mind your own business!" She tried to grab Alex's notebook from him, but he pulled it away.

"Oh, that's okay," Tina replied, standing between Alex and Gaby. She felt like a referee in a boxing ring. The brother and sister were squared off for a real live match and Tina didn't want to get caught in the middle. Jamal came over and pushed the pair apart.

"C'mon, you guys, let's not get into a fight over this," he said, as Tina looked at him with a smile of appreciation.

"Listen," Alex said. "This stolen backpack stuff's a mystery, a case. And a good detective always writes things down like suspects and evidence." He pointed to the tall stack of detective novels on the night table on his side of the room. "I read about it all the time," he told Tina.

Gaby rolled her eyes. "Who said *you're* a good detective?" she asked sarcastically.

Alex glared at his sister. This was no way to impress a cute girl like Tina.

"Hey, cool! A casebook," Tina said, trying to defuse the explosive atmosphere.

"Yeah, a casebook," Alex repeated casually. "I'll show you how to make one sometime."

"Okay." Tina smiled. "Well, I've got to go. Thanks again, Gaby."

"Sure," Gaby said.

"Good luck, detective," Tina said, smiling at Alex.

"Thanks," he mumbled, embarrassed. "I'll see you later." He watched as Tina waved and went out the door.

Now Gaby giggled from her side of the room as she watched Alex watching Tina.

"What's so funny?" Alex asked defensively.

"He likes her," she teased, looking at Jamal as she pushed back the sheet dividing the room. "He likes her!"

"Who?" Alex asked, feeling himself start to blush again.

Gaby looked at Jamal and smiled. "He knows who I mean," she said.

"No, I don't know," Alex growled.

"Yes, you do. I can see it in your eyes," she said, laughing.

"Yeah, well, see this, why don't you," he shouted as he pulled the divider closed.

Jamal watched the brother and sister and snickered.

"Hey, sorry, man," Jamal said, putting his hands up and backing toward Alex's bed. "I'm not in this thing."

"Look," Alex said, changing the subject. "We've got to stick to this mask clue."

"Yeah, it looks like all the thieves were wearing the same double masks. I wonder where they got them," Jamal said.

"What kind of store would sell stuff like that?" Alex asked.

"Wait a minute!" Jamal shouted, jumping up and reaching into his pocket.

He took out the THABTO button and turned it over.

"How about a store that would sell buttons like this?" he asked. "Look at that, The Party Animal logo!" He pointed to the sticker of the cat wearing a party hat.

"It's been right under our noses," Alex said. "That store called The Party Animal downtown! Let's go!"

Alex grabbed his casebook and the boys dashed out.

They quickly walked to the main street, passing the bakery, the drugstore, the stationery store, and the jeweler's.

"Where is this place?" Jamal asked, looking around.

"Next block," Alex said as he pointed ahead. "I know the kid whose folks own the place. A real slimeball," he said as they walked. "He has this pet parrot he named Attila. It's the most annoying pet I've ever seen. They keep it in the store, if you can believe that one!"

"A parrot?" Jamal asked. "This I have got to see."

"This is it," Alex said, leading Jamal inside a store with a large green awning that read THE PARTY ANIMAL.

The store was filled with multicolored balloons stamped with the logo of a cat wearing a party hat, the same logo on the button Jamal had found.

Behind the counter, Alex spotted Calvin Ferguson and his pet parrot.

"*Qué pasa,* Alex?" Calvin said in a loud, nasty voice. "How'd you do on that social studies test? I got a one hundred and five! Extra-credit question!" he bragged.

"*Aarrk!* You're brilliant, Calvin!" the parrot screeched.

"What's *with* this bozo?" Jamal whispered to Alex.

Alex shrugged. "He's in some of my classes."

"Aren't you going to introduce me to your friend, Alex?" Calvin called.

"Jamal Jenkins," Alex muttered.

Jamal smiled.

"Wussup, homey?" Calvin said. He sneered and looked at Jamal suspiciously.

Jamal clenched his fist. "Is your bird real? Or is there a tape recorder in there?" he asked, smirking at Calvin.

Alex tugged Jamal away. "Ignore that jerk. Let's look around. That's what we came here for."

The boys searched among the displays of cards, knick-knacks, puzzles, stationery, balloons, and trinkets. Suddenly Jamal spotted a basket of creepy full-headed, double-faced masks.

"That's what I saw in the park!" he whispered to Alex.

Alex picked up one of the thick rubber masks and gave it a closer look.

"The thieves must have bought their masks from here," Jamal said.

Alex nodded, then walked to a button display rack. "Look at this!" he said. He pointed to a sign that read BUTTONS TO ORDER—YOU THINK IT, WE MAKE IT!

"This is solid evidence. We should write this in our casebook," Alex said.

He opened his casebook and wrote: "The Party Animal sells THABTO buttons *and* double masks."

The words suddenly glimmered and glowed a bright yellow on the page.

"Ghostwriter!" Alex whispered.

"He's on the case!" Jamal said, watching the swirling words.

Jamal took the THABTO button from his pocket. He and Alex walked to the counter, where Calvin stood behind the register.

"*Aarrk!* Your public awaits, Calvin!" the parrot squealed.

Calvin flashed a halfhearted smile.

"Do you know who ordered this?" Jamal asked, holding the button up to Calvin.

"I can't give you information like that," Calvin sniffed. "It's confidential."

Jamal shook his head. His attention was caught by a sudden glow on a sign in the store. "Hey! Alex, look!" he said, pointing to the sign, which read:

THADNUNK'S TRUSTY TAGS, BOX OF 10—$6.95
BOX OF 25—$16.50

The glowing yellow light shimmered and the letters moved around as Ghostwriter gave a message to Alex and Jamal:

THABTO FOUR BUTTONS DAN 555-1966

"Get that down, man!" Jamal said.

Calvin had looked at the sign along with the boys but could not see the letters moving. "Get what down?" he said, looking confused.

Alex scribbled the name and number in his casebook as Calvin tried to look over his shoulder.

He turned and looked at the sign, which Ghostwriter had returned to normal, and shrugged.

"I think we're all set. Thanks, Calvin," Alex said as the

boys dashed from the store. They raced around the corner, laughing hysterically, and flopped against a wall. They held their sides until they ached from laughing.

"*Aarrk!* He's helpful!" Jamal imitated the shrieking parrot.

"*Aarrk!* He's charming!" Alex sputtered.

"*Aarrk!* What a birdbrain!" Jamal gasped. The boys walked down the street and plopped onto a bus stop bench. Alex opened his casebook. He and Jamal pored over Ghostwriter's message: THABTO FOUR BUT-TONS DAN 555-1966

"Ghostwriter must have read this somewhere in the store," Alex said as Jamal pointed to the telephone number.

"You know, you leave your phone number when you place a special order," Alex said.

Jamal nodded. "I did that once with a new computer game. They called me when it came in."

"So maybe somebody named Dan ordered four buttons with THABTO printed on them," Alex suggested.

Jamal jumped up. "Let's go," he shouted. "We have got to tell Lenni!"

The boys raced excitedly to Lenni's house and rang the intercom at the bottom of the stairs to the loft. No answer. They rang again, pressing hard on the buzzer and holding it down for longer than necessary.

"Where could she be?" Alex asked impatiently.

"It's Sunday." Jamal sighed. "She could be anywhere. Maybe she went out with her dad or something."

"I think her dad had a show to do today," Alex said. "Maybe she went to watch."

The dejected pair was about to leave when the buzzer suddenly rang.

They rang the bell again. "Lenni?" they called into the intercom.

"Hi. Sorry. I was on the phone," she called down. "I'll buzz you in."

The boys raced up the stairs to the loft and excitedly told Lenni about their trip to the party store.

"So you think we should call this Dan guy?" she asked.

"Definitely!" Alex said, pacing the room. "But how are we gonna get him to tell us what THABTO means?"

Jamal grimaced. "Alex is right. If he's one of the backpack thieves, he's not just going to volunteer the information."

"Maybe we can say we're from The Party Animal store and we need information for our mailing records," Alex said, brightening.

"I could pretend to be Calvin," Jamal offered.

"And I'll be the bird!" Alex laughed. "*Aarrk!* You're lame, Calvin!"

Jamal went to the phone.

"See if you can get his whole name," Lenni suggested as Jamal dialed the number. She tried to think of all the boys she knew named Dan. None of them would be the kind of kid to steal backpacks, she thought. But Dan was a popular name. There was no telling how many Dans there were at her school.

"Ask him what THABTO means," Alex added.

"And his address," Lenni said.

"And see if you can find out what the double mask is for," Alex advised.

Jamal put his hand over the phone. "Shhhh! Hold it, you guys! I've got to think!" He cleared his throat. Trying to sound like Calvin, Jamal spoke into the phone.

"Hello, Dan? This is Calvin Ferguson, from The Party Animal."

"*Aarrk!* You're brilliant, Calvin," Alex chirped in the background.

Jamal rolled his eyes at Alex and continued speaking into the phone. "We're just updating our mailing list and we'd like to get your full name and address . . . Oh, okay." He covered the phone with one hand.

"He doesn't want to be on our mailing list," Jamal informed his anxious friends.

"Ask him about THABTO," Lenni whispered.

"Well, okay, Dan," Jamal continued. "One more thing, though. You remember that button you ordered, don't you . . . Yes, well, it was so strange and interesting that we wanted to know exactly what does THABTO mean, for our records, you know. Just in case you wanted to order any more . . ."

Jamal sighed and slammed the phone down.

"Well, that was a bust," he said.

"What'd he say?" Alex asked.

"He said he doesn't want to order any more because there are only four members on his team. Then he hung up. *Nothing!*"

Lenni jumped up.

"What do you mean 'nothing'?" she shouted. "Jamal, that was great detective work! We know two things now that we didn't know before: that THABTO is a team *and* that there are only four members!"

The trio all started talking at once.

"Wait, you guys," Lenni shouted. "This deserves the secret handshake!"

"Right!" Jamal beamed, feeling better after Lenni's compliment. He shook Lenni's, then Alex's hand. Alex and Lenni did the same.

"Now what?" Alex asked as he slumped onto the couch. Lenni crawled into her favorite blue chair.

"Now," she said, smiling happily, "we think!"

CHAPTER 9

Crowds of students jammed the halls of Hurston Middle School as Alex and Lenni walked into the building Monday morning. Four boys wearing blue-and-white varsity letter jackets walked down the hall, talking quietly.

"Did you see those four guys wearing the same jackets?" Lenni gasped as the group walked by.

"Lenni! They're on the basketball team. Chill out!" Alex said, laughing.

Lenni sighed. "My brain's getting fried from trying to find those THABTOs. When I see four of anything I think that might be them."

Alex slowed down as they walked through the hall and

turned toward a large bulletin board. "Lenni, look!" he whispered. The glow of Ghostwriter glimmered as letters rearranged themselves on the bulletin board to spell out a bright red message:

PENCO PRODUCTS, INC., 163
THABTO

Lenni read the message out loud, looking around nervously to see if anyone in the hallway had seen the glowing red letters. Other kids hung out in the hall, talking and fooling around. No one noticed the message from Ghostwriter to Lenni and Alex.

"Ghostwriter's trying to send us a message about a THABTO," she whispered to Alex.

"Penco Products," Alex said, scratching his head. "Where have I seen that before? It sounds so familiar!"

"I'll ask him what he means," Lenni said, pulling out a page from her notebook.

"What do you mean?" Lenni wrote on the page to Ghostwriter.

Ghostwriter did not reply.

"I guess he doesn't know," Alex said. They stopped in front of his locker.

Just then Alex spotted it. He grabbed Lenni's arm and pointed to the row of lockers lining the hall. Each one had a small metal plate that said PENCO PRODUCTS, INC. and a locker number.

"A locker number, Lenni," Alex nearly shouted. "A locker number, that's what Ghostwriter gave us!"

They stood before Alex's locker, number 174.

"The locker number of a THABTO team member," Lenni said, looking down the hall. "All we have to do is find 163."

"The numbers go this way," Alex said, pulling her down the hall. "Come on!"

Alex's locker was at the end of the hall. They turned left and followed the numbers just as the class bell rang and crowds of kids pushed and shoved their way to class.

They stopped a short way down the hall.

"Here it is," Alex whispered, peering around.

"Whose locker is it?" Lenni asked. Alex shrugged and shook his head. They looked down the hallway as a group of kids approached, slowed down, then walked past the locker.

The late bell jangled.

"We better move it," Alex said. "I'm already late for social studies. I'll see you outside after school."

"Okay," Lenni said, dashing off to her English class.

Between classes Alex went out of his way to pass locker 163. He didn't see anyone go near it. At 3:15 he met Lenni in the schoolyard.

"I must have cased that locker all day," Alex said. "I waited around at lunchtime *and* after class. I didn't see anybody! Not a single clue."

"Maybe the person left school early," Lenni said.

"Yeah, to rob some poor little kids," Alex grumbled.

"I hope Jamal had better luck with the school secretary," Lenni said, looking for their friend in the crowds. She spotted Jamal racing out the front door and down the steps.

"Well?" Alex asked expectantly.

Jamal shook his head. "Nothing," he said, frowning. "The secretary wouldn't give me one sixty-three's name. And I used all my wit and charm to try to get it, too!"

"No wonder you came up cold," Alex said, punching Jamal playfully.

"A dead end," Lenni sighed.

"We gave it a shot," Jamal said. "We're just going to have to keep an eye on that locker. In the meantime we'll keep trying to crack that code."

"I'm for that," Lenni said, pulling her backpack onto her shoulder.

"Me too," Alex said. "But first I've got to pick up Gaby from school."

"Let's go," Jamal said. "We'll keep you company."

"Great!" Alex said, feeling better for the first time all day.

They crossed the street and took a shortcut through the park to the elementary school a few blocks away.

"There she is!" Lenni said, spotting Gaby in the crowd and waving to her. Gaby trotted over.

"Hi, guys," Gaby said. "This is great! Thanks for picking me up. Come back to our house and I'll tell you what's going on with the robberies. Mama is making her special chocolate cake today, too."

"Sounds great," Jamal said, suddenly hungry and picturing a fudgy homemade treat.

Alex, Gaby, Jamal, and Lenni walked up to the bodega minutes later.

"Tina showed her video about the backpack robbers at a special school assembly today," Gaby told the kids as they

74

entered the store. "The principal told everybody that we have to be very careful."

Mr. Fernandez, who was behind the counter at the cash register, heard Gaby.

"It's a terrible thing when children cannot even walk safely to school," he said, shaking his head in disgust.

"Hi, Mr. Fernandez," Lenni and Jamal said. "*Hola, Papa*," Gaby and Alex greeted him.

"Don't worry, Papa, I feel very safe with Alex," Gaby said, giving her brother a you-owe-me-one grin. "And today I had Jamal and Lenni, too!"

"That's what big brothers are for," Mr. Fernandez said, looking straight at Alex. He went to the refrigerated section and started to unpack a delivery of fresh eggs.

"Your mama left chocolate cake in the kitchen," he said. "Go, enjoy!"

Alex turned to Lenni and Jamal. "Let's hit the cake. Then we've got to crack that coded message," he said.

"What coded message?" Gaby asked curiously. Alex, Jamal, and Lenni felt guilty as they looked at Gaby, but no one said a word. Jamal and Lenni followed Alex to the apartment behind the bodega. Gaby trotted along behind them. "What coded message?" she repeated.

"Never mind, Gaby," Alex said, hoping to dismiss her.

"All right then, don't tell me. And I won't tell *you*," Gaby said. She stood waiting for their reaction as she took a light-blue piece of paper out of her lunchbox.

"But maybe after you crack *your* coded message, you could help me crack the coded message that I got," she said.

"You got a coded message?" Alex asked.

"Where did you find it?" asked Lenni.

"Can we see it?" Jamal asked.

"Weeeell, I don't know," Gaby said. She sauntered past Alex, Lenni, and Jamal. They followed her meekly into the bedroom.

Alex smiled affectionately and put his arm around her shoulder. "Gaby, old pal, old chum. My favorite sister," he said, reaching for the message.

"Don't try to butter me up!" she said.

"We really have to see that," Jamal said nicely. "It could be important, Gaby. You could really help us with this case."

Gaby looked at the three anxious faces.

"Oh, all right," she said, handing the paper over to Jamal. The kids crowded around to look at the message:

ARNG NAQ PYRNA V TBG NJNL
URL URL

"Where'd you get this?" Lenni asked again.

"It was weird," Gaby said. "I found it in my trivia book in my backpack when I got to school this morning."

"How'd it get there?" Jamal asked.

"It was left by the thief," Gaby said. "And it turns out that everybody who found their stolen backpacks found the same weird note! I've been trying to figure it out all day."

Jamal handed the message back to Gaby and she put it

on Alex's desk next to the note Jamal had found in the park. The four kids stood around and tried to make sense out of the two coded messages.

The one Jamal found:

ZRRGVAT SEVQNL FRCGRZORE GJRYSGU
GUR SVANY FRPERG PRERZBAL
ORTVAF ERAEBP LINA QENL

And Gaby's:

ARNG NAQ PYRNA V TBG NJNL
URL URL

"Now that we have two messages, what can we figure out?" Alex asked.

"One thing we know pretty much for sure," Lenni said. "Both messages are from THABTO."

"How do we know that?" Gaby asked.

"First of all, both are written on the same kind of blue paper in the same kind of lettering," Lenni explained.

The four leaned closer to the messages on the desktop.

"And second," she continued, "Jamal found his message right next to a THABTO button and you found yours in your backpack, which was probably stolen by a THABTO!"

"All right," Gaby agreed. "But what do they say?"

"We don't know yet. They're in code," Alex said.

"But they can't be in a code where the letters are scrambled," Jamal pointed out, "because we already tried that."

"So we figure this must be a code where one letter stands for another letter," Alex concluded.

"Okay, let's get moving," Lenni said impatiently. "What do we do first?"

Gaby pointed to the letter *V* in her message. "See this letter? This must be an *I* or an *A*," she said.

"Why do you think that?" Lenni asked.

"Because it's a one-letter word. And in English the only words that have just one letter are *I* and *A*."

"Fourteen, fifteen, sixteen, seventeen. Look," Alex said. "I've counted seventeen *R*s in the two messages. That's more than any other letter!"

"How's that going to help?" Jamal asked.

"Because *E* is the letter used most in the English language," Alex said. "*R* might be *E* in the code."

Alex took out a piece of paper. "I'm going to try something," he said, as he wrote the twenty-six letters of the alphabet across the paper.

A B C D E F G H I J K L M N O P Q R S T U V W X Y Z

"Now, if *R* stands for *E*, then *S* stands for *F*," Alex said, and began filling in the rest of the alphabet.

"Hey," Lenni said, "the *V* is an *I*."

"I knew it!" Gaby beamed.

"So Alex, what happens when you get to the *Z*?" Jamal asked.

"You just go to the beginning and write the rest of the letters," he explained. "*N, O, P,* and all the rest!"

He continued writing. "All done!" he announced and held up the piece of paper to his friends.

A	B	C	D	E	F	G	H	I	J	K	L	M
N	O	P	Q	R	S	T	U	V	W	X	Y	Z

N	O	P	Q	R	S	T	U	V	W	X	Y	Z
A	B	C	D	E	F	G	H	I	J	K	L	M

They stared at the two rows of letters. "Let's see how it works with the messages," Jamal said.

"I'm getting something already," Alex said excitedly as he started to copy the coded letters.

"Me too!" Gaby gasped. "*B* is *O* and the *G* is a *T* . . . *'GOT'*!"

They substituted all the letters until both messages were decoded.

The message Jamal found in the park read:

MEETING FRIDAY, SEPTEMBER TWELFTH
THE FINAL SECRET CEREMONY
BEGINS RENROC YVAN DRAY

Gaby's message read:

NEAT AND CLEAN I GOT AWAY
HEY HEY

"We did it," Alex said.

"We cracked the code!" Lenni cheered.

Gaby looked down at her decoded message and smirked. "Hey, hey, you *creeps.* I can't wait to get my hands on that THABTO. He stole my money and I want it back!"

Jamal reread the message he'd found: "'Meeting Friday, September twelfth. The final secret ceremony.' Secret ceremony? I must have seen one of their secret ceremonies in the park last week!"

"September twelfth is this Friday," Lenni said, looking at the calendar on the wall. "But it doesn't say what time or where."

"It must be in those last three words," Alex said, pointing to the words in the last line that read "renroc yvan dray."

"What does that mean?" Gaby asked.

They looked at one another and shrugged. "Must be another kind of code," Alex said.

"Another code." Jamal and Lenni groaned.

"It took us four days to crack the first one," Jamal said.

"And the secret ceremony is only three days away," Lenni added.

Gaby rubbed her eyes and walked to her side of the room. "All this code stuff's made my eyes hurt," she said, flopping onto her bed.

Alex signaled to Jamal and Lenni to come closer. "Maybe we can ask Ghostwriter if he can help us some more," he whispered.

Jamal nodded as Alex pointed toward Gaby's side of the room. "Whatever we want him to do, we've got to write it down so he can read it because he can't hear us," he whispered back, taking Alex's cue.

"How can we write to Ghostwriter with Gaby nosing into everything we do?" Alex asked.

Gaby's sudden shriek interrupted their whispered conversation. Alex pushed aside the room-dividing sheet.

"What's wrong?" he cried.

Gaby stared and pointed at her bulletin board. "Th-th-that!" she stuttered, pointing to words glimmering in yellow letters on the otherwise bare bulletin board.

"What is that?"

Ghostwriter's message, written from letters found on other places in the room, read: GABY THIRSTS FOR NO LEDGE.

Lenni read the message. "'Gaby thirsts for no ledge?'"

With the sheet no longer dividing the room, Ghostwriter lifted the letters *K* and *W* from posters and signs on Alex's side of the room to complete the message.

GABY THIRSTS FOR KNOWLEDGE.

Gaby continued to stare, dumbfounded, at the glowing letters.

"'Gaby thirsts for knowledge?'" Jamal said, reading the sign.

"Sure," Alex laughed. "You know. Like she always wants to know stuff!"

"Gaby . . . Gaby . . . ," Lenni said, taking the frightened

little girl by the hand. "Let's fill you in on *all* the details of the case. Maybe we could go in the kitchen and have a piece of that chocolate cake now. It's time we introduced you to our new friend . . . Ghostwriter!"

CHAPTER 10

The school day seemed to last forever. Alex bolted from his seat as the last bell rang and headed for the hallway near locker 163.

He paced back and forth in the hall around the corner, poking his head out every so often to see if anyone came by to use the locker.

After several minutes he turned to go, then spotted a boy carrying a couple of books heading straight for locker 163. Alex walked to the water fountain and pretended to take a drink.

He glanced up as the boy opened the locker, shoved in the books, and slammed it closed.

"I know I've seen that kid somewhere," Alex said to

himself, trying to remember where. He followed the boy down the hall, out of the building, and down the street. The boy walked along happily, unaware he was being followed. Alex felt like a real detective. For two blocks Alex shadowed the boy, straight to the video arcade.

Alex bent to tie his shoe as he watched the kid walk inside.

He peered through the window. He saw the kid from locker 163 head straight for the Double Defenders video game, where he met two boys and a girl.

"That's where I remember him from!" Alex said to himself as he walked into the arcade. "The day I met Jamal here, they were playing that game!"

Loud rock music and the sound of video-game bells and beeps filled the crowded arcade. Kids were cheering each other on as the contests heated up in the hot, dark arcade. Boys and girls pushed and shoved to get closer to the machines and the regular big-time players.

Alex walked to a nearby game. He tried to look casual as he snuck glances at the foursome around the Double Defenders machine.

These guys are serious, he thought as he watched them get lost in the frenzy of the game. Alex stood for several minutes, fascinated by the fierce competition. He noticed something about the four players. They all wore army belts and denim jackets. He took out his casebook and jotted some notes as the noise and music blasted louder and louder in the background.

The four gathered tightly around the machine, which

featured a colorful display of the two-headed, double-jointed superheroes.

Above the machine was a sign announcing: DOUBLE DEFENDERS TOURNAMENT, SATURDAY, SEPTEMBER 13TH, AT 12 NOON. Alex scribbled furiously in his casebook, hoping not to be noticed.

As he wrote the last word he looked up, startled by the sound of the players screaming directions to each other.

"Behind you, behind you!" one kid yelled.

"Double-jam that monster slime, Great Gripper. Double-jam him!" another shouted.

"Don't worry, Masher, I've got him double-twisted!"

Alex listened in disbelief as the players entered the world of Double Defenders.

"Hey, those names," he said to himself.

"Watch out!" one kid shrieked. "Your other head!"

"In your face, slimeball," his partner screamed back.

"Out of the way, Rocket Ripper," the kid ordered.

"All right, Kicker. Double-joint 'em," Rocket Ripper said, moving aside.

The shouts, cheers, and jeers continued as the game got hotter and hotter. Alex wrote the names of the superheroes in his casebook, looked at the four wild-eyed players again, and hurried out of the arcade.

Alex found Lenni, Jamal, and Gaby waiting for him in his room.

"Locker number one sixty-three likes to hang out at the video arcade after school," he reported.

"And those weird names sound like something that girl told me about when I interviewed her," Gaby said.

Alex looked at his sister. "What? You interviewed someone else whose backpack was stolen?"

"Yes," she said, getting out her notebook. "I wrote it down." Gaby read the account out loud: "'The thief's double mask fell off. Then somebody yelled to the thief, "Run, Rocket Ripper, run!"'"

Alex, Lenni, and Jamal looked at each other in surprise.

"A backpack thief called Rocket Ripper?" Lenni asked.

Alex checked his casebook. "That's one of the names from that Double Defenders video game—and those kids who were playing kept calling each other those weird names—Rocket Ripper, Great Gripper, Mighty Masher, Kool Kicker," he said.

"So you're saying the Double Defenders people are the same ones who stole the backpacks?" Gaby asked.

"It makes sense," Jamal said. "Those thieves were wearing double masks. Maybe they were trying to look like two-headed Double Defenders heroes."

"I just thought of something else," Lenni added. "We know there were four thieves because they made up four THABTO buttons. And there were four Double Defenders players."

Alex jumped to his feet. "It's got to be the same people."

Lenni nodded in agreement. "Right, if only we could prove it. We need to catch them in the act."

"Or crack that second code," Alex said.

Gaby and Lenni sighed.

"Wait a minute," Jamal said. "I've got an idea. Don't they have books and stuff on Double Defenders?"

"They must," Lenni said. "It's a whole imaginary world with weird characters and made-up planets."

"So maybe the THABTOs got their ideas from the books," Jamal said. "I'm going to check it out." Jamal grabbed his backpack. "I'll talk to you guys later if I find out anything we can use."

Jamal stopped at the library on his way home.

"How can I find information on Double Defenders?" Jamal asked the librarian. "It's a video game," he added in response to her puzzled look.

The librarian pointed Jamal toward a corner of the library where he could find books on games. He scanned the titles and found a thin paperback book about Double Defenders.

"Success!" said the librarian with a friendly smile as she checked out Jamal's find.

He walked the few blocks to his house excitedly, hopeful that he could find the missing pieces of the puzzle.

When he got home, he found a note in the living room from Grandma CeCe: "Went to the store. Be back soon. Have a snack. Love, Grandma."

Jamal smiled. *Grandma CeCe and her snacks,* he thought. He was too excited to eat. He headed up to his room and took out a pad of blank paper and a sharp pencil. Jamal stretched out on his bed, looking at the nearly decoded message.

MEETING FRIDAY, SEPTEMBER TWELFTH
THE FINAL SECRET CEREMONY
BEGINS RENROC YVAN DRAY

He read the words out loud and circled the final three coded words.

"What could that be?" he cried in frustration.

He put the message next to the pad, picked up the Double Defenders book, and started reading.

Princess Helena of Katelisa had a friend, the sometimes wizard, Ethan Gumption III, whose father had been a confidant to King Quatrain until the mad king . . .

Oh, man, this is worse than math, Jamal thought, slamming the book shut. *How can people keep it all straight?*

Jamal jumped up, throwing the book onto the bed, and walked over to his computer. He flicked it on and started writing.

"Ghostwriter, I need help," he typed.

HELP JAMAL, Ghostwriter wrote on the screen.

"No, I need real help," Jamal typed.

HELP JAMAL! the screen answered.

"Thanks for nothing," Jamal muttered. He pushed his chair from the computer, and, tired and frustrated, flopped onto his bed, shoving the book and pad to the floor.

CHAPTER 11

Loud jazz music from the stereo rocked the rafters in Lenni's loft. Max sat at his drums and played along, pounding a rhythmic beat. Lenni sat on a stool watching.

She looked across the floor of the big open-spaced loft and held her breath. Ghostwriter had rearranged the magnetic plastic letters on the refrigerator door. He was sending her a message!

HELP JAMAL! the letters spelled. Lenni forgot for the moment that her dad was nearby. "What's the matter with Jamal?" she said.

"Excuse me?" Max shouted over the music.

Lenni rushed to the telephone without answering.

* * *

At the same moment, Alex was working in the bodega, putting cans on shelves. Mr. Fernandez was proudly inspecting the new flower display he had set up earlier that day.

Alex gasped as he spotted a box of Jolly Jack's Pirate Munch cereal across the aisle, glowing orange. The glow jumped to a second box and the letters moved around. A message appeared: HELP JAMAL!

Gaby rushed into the store and over to Alex.

"Did you just get a message from Ghostwriter?" she whispered.

"Yeah," Alex whispered back. "Let's go call Jamal."

In her loft, Lenni dialed and redialed Jamal's house, getting a busy signal each time. Max drummed a smooth, softer version of the same song in the background. After the third try and busy signal, Lenni slammed down the phone.

"Dad, can I go over to Jamal's house for a minute?" she asked as she headed toward the door.

"There's school tomorrow, Bips," he said, stopping his drumming.

"Please, Dad. It's really important," Lenni begged.

Max hesitated. "Well, all right. Don't stay long, though," he said, picking up the beat as she dashed out the door.

Lenni raced down the stairs and flung open the door to the street, nearly knocking down Alex and Gaby.

"Did you guys get the message, too?" she asked. They nodded and followed her closely as she raced toward Jamal's house.

Jamal was lying on his bed, flipping a pen up in the air and catching it, when he heard a knock at his door.

"Who is it?" he asked.

"Us," came a breathless chorus of Lenni, Alex, and Gaby. "Open the door!"

Jamal jumped from his bed and pulled open the door.

"What are you guys doing here?" he asked, looking from one to the other in total confusion.

"Are you okay? What's wrong?" The three all babbled at once.

"I'm fine. What's up?" Jamal asked, shaking his head.

"Ghostwriter sent each of us a message to 'Help Jamal!'" Gaby explained.

"That's strange," Jamal said as he walked over to his computer. "I mean, I did write to him that I needed help but . . ."

He stopped and looked at the computer. "So that's why he kept on writing back 'Help Jamal!'"

"Wow!" Alex cried, plopping onto Jamal's bed. "He sent each one of us a message from you!"

"Jeepers!" Jamal laughed. "And I just thought Ghostwriter was being dense."

"This is so cool," Lenni said excitedly. "I don't think we have to worry about Ghostwriter ever being dense!"

"It's kind of like being beamed up," Gaby said, laughing.

"Better than the telephone," Alex said, jumping up. "Because we can communicate no matter where we are!"

"We should make up a special word that we can use when we need help or we need everybody to come over," Lenni suggested.

They tossed around a bunch of names, code words, and signals that they could use to have Ghostwriter summon them as a group. Alex suggested *Yo,* but Jamal didn't like that one and came up with *Flash.* Code names flew through the air. Gaby came up with *Fly,* but that was rejected.

"Boogie," Lenni said.

"Yuck!" Gaby made a face. "That sounds like *booger!*" All the kids cracked up.

"Wait," Jamal said. "I've got it. *Rally.*"

"Like in *stock car rally,*" Alex piped up.

Gaby shook her head in disagreement. "I don't know. We're not cars."

"I like *Rally,* too," Lenni said.

"Well, what does *rally* mean anyway?" Gaby asked.

"It means to get together," Jamal explained.

"Sort of like a call to action," Alex added.

All eyes were on Gaby as she listened to their explanations.

"Oh, I get it," she said. *"Rally."*

"Rally it is!" Jamal said as he put his hand out and they all did their Ghostwriter handshake.

The kids sat around Jamal's room, talking about how

Ghostwriter had contacted each one of them for the first time.

"I wonder why he picked us?" Lenni asked. "It's not like we really knew each other well from school."

"Maybe we have some special powers we don't know about," Alex said, his eyes glowing with excitement.

"I don't think we have special powers," Jamal said. "But Ghostwriter certainly does. He must have picked us because we could help him use them in a good way. If he helps us solve this backpack mystery we'll have started something special."

They nodded and sat silently, thinking about their first impressions of Ghostwriter.

"I think there's one more thing we should do," Jamal said, getting everyone's attention and returning to the original subject. "When we write *rally* we should write the first letter of our first name so that you know who's calling it. Like if it's me I'll write *Rally J,* and you all will know to come here."

"All right, *Rally J,*" Alex said. "Now we're all here. Why'd you call?"

"Check out my bed," Jamal said, pointing to the Double Defenders book and the message with the last line still in code. "I'm up to my eyeballs in this Double Defenders stuff."

Lenni picked up the message. "If we can just figure out these last three words we'll know when the secret ceremony begins," she said.

The gang looked over her shoulder at the message:

MEETING FRIDAY, SEPTEMBER TWELFTH
THE FINAL SECRET CEREMONY
BEGINS RENROC YVAN DRAY

They shook their heads.

"Look," Alex said. "Why don't we all split up? Lenni and I can work on decoding those words. Jamal, you and Gaby can keep studying the book."

"Thanks a lot, pal," Jamal teased. "This book is like reading a foreign language!"

"Come on, Jamal," Gaby said, pulling him by the arm. "We can do that. We'll show them!"

Gaby and Jamal plunged into the Double Defenders book. Alex and Lenni pored over the meeting announcement.

Lenni picked up a pencil. "Maybe we can move the letters around. Like this . . . ," she said as she wrote *ANY* under *YVAN*.

"No good," Alex said. "That leaves the *V* left over."

"You're right," she said, erasing the *ANY*.

"But what if we change the letters around by just reversing them?" Lenni said excitedly.

Alex wrote the word *CORNER* under *RENROC*.

"Hey, *corner*! I think you've got something," he cried, slapping Lenni on the back.

"And that uses all the letters in that one," Lenni said.

"Then we've got it," Alex said as he wrote *NAVY* under *YVAN* and *YARD* under *DRAY*.

"Corner Navy Yard!" Lenni shouted.

"You did it!" Alex said, putting out his hand for the Ghostwriter handshake.

"*We* did it!" Lenni smiled. "Hey, guys," she called to Jamal and Gaby. "We did it! We just reversed the order of the letters in the last three words."

"You were right, Gaby," Alex admitted. "It was staring us right in the face."

"Listen to this," Lenni said, clearing her throat as she officially read the message: "Meeting Friday, September twelfth. The final secret ceremony begins. Corner Navy Yard."

"Great," Jamal said. "Now we know where it is."

"Yes," Gaby said. "But . . . *when* is it?"

Lenni's smile vanished. "Oh no!" she moaned.

"Looks like we're back to that Double Defenders book again," Jamal said.

"Hey, wait a minute," Alex said. "Maybe Ghostwriter can help us now."

"How?" Lenni asked, slumping on Jamal's bed, her excitement deflated.

"By helping us read through this book," Alex explained.

"Why not?" Jamal said as he sat at the computer.

The others followed and stood around as Jamal began typing.

"When do the Double Defenders meet? Can you help us read?" Jamal said out loud as he typed it onto the screen.

I'LL FLY THROUGH THE WORDS! Ghostwriter responded.

The kids turned to the book on Jamal's bed.

They watched as Ghostwriter's green glow zoomed through it.

"Oh, wow!" Gaby shouted in amazement.

"Now that's what I call speed reading!" Alex said.

The glow bounced around the book for a few moments. Jamal turned to the computer.

"Wait! Something's coming up on the screen," he said.

Jamal read out loud as Ghostwriter wrote: THE ART OF DOUBLE DEFENSE, PAGE 189.

"I'll get it," Alex said. He leafed through the book and found page 189.

"This might be it," he said. He started reading out loud. "'The Double Defenders superheroes hold secret meetings after high noon. They find out about them through a secret message. The time is determined by counting the number of words in the first two lines and then subtracting one.'"

Jamal grabbed the message and began counting, "One, two, three, four, five, six, seven, eight. So eight minus one equals seven."

"This Friday at seven P.M. in a corner of the Navy Yard!" Lenni said, as they cheered and hugged each other.

"Now maybe we can get some proof straight up that the THABTOs are the backpack thieves," Alex said.

"How?" Jamal asked. "By crashing their ceremony?"

"Why not?" Alex said slyly. "I'll go in disguise as one of them."

"But they'd know," Gaby said. "You'd be an extra guy."

"Not if I go as the kid from locker number one sixty-three," he pointed out.

"But how will we keep him away from the ceremony?" Lenni asked.

Alex wrinkled his brow as he thought out loud. "We'll write him a note telling him that the ceremony's been canceled. We'll write it in their code. On light-blue paper. And then we'll stick it in his locker," he said.

Jamal smiled with a gleam in his eye. "I like that," he said. "I like that a lot."

CHAPTER 12

The next afternoon, Jamal went to Lenni's loft to plan their strategy for spying on the Double Defenders. Alex and Gaby were working in the bodega downstairs.

"Now what exactly are we going to say in the note to this THABTO kid?" Jamal asked. He was sprawled out on Lenni's couch, looking through her father's prized collection of old jazz albums.

"Well, we have to keep him away from their final ceremony tomorrow," Lenni reminded him. "So let's just say that it's canceled, like Alex said."

"Okay," Jamal agreed. "How about, 'Our final ceremony is off for now'?"

"That's good," Lenni said, starting to write. "Wait a minute. What if he mentions it to one of the other THABTOs? Then he'll know he got tricked."

"Maybe we should tell him not to speak to any of them," Jamal suggested.

"Okay," Lenni nodded. "But make it sound important. Like it's part of the THABTO thing."

"Right," Jamal agreed.

"'Don't get in touch,'" Lenni started. "No. That's not official enough. 'You must make no contact with others . . . '"

"'Until you receive further notice,'" Jamal added.

Lenni wrote it down. "That's good," she said. "Then we could end with: 'This is absolutely top secret.'"

"'Absolutely, positively top secret,'" Jamal emphasized.

Lenni finished writing the message. "Okay," she said, handing the message to Jamal.

"Here goes," he said, reading it out loud: "'Our final ceremony is off for now. You must make no contact with others until you receive further notice. This is absolutely, positively top secret.'"

"That should do it," Jamal said. "Let's put it into code."

Lenni picked up the message and read it over again. "It's much too long. It will take forever to get it into code," she said. "Let's see what words we can leave out without losing the important stuff."

They looked through the message, crossing out extra words. Soon each word in the message gave important information.

Lenni read the new, shorter message: "'Ceremony is off.

Make no contact with others until further notice. Top secret.'"

"We did it. And it still says everything we want it to say," Lenni said.

"Great. Now let's put it in code," Jamal said.

They looked at the message they had written on a piece of light-blue paper:

PRERZBA VF BSS. ZNXR AB PBAGNPG JVGU
BGUREF
HAGVY SHEGURE ABGVPR. GBC FRPERG

"We better get over to school and put this in the locker so number one sixty-three knows not to come," Lenni said.

"You're right," Jamal agreed, grabbing his backpack. "We'll make it just in time to get into school before the janitors lock up for the night."

They hurried out of Lenni's loft and down the stairs. Lenni poked her head into the bodega, where she spotted Alex and Gaby.

"Hi, guys," she called. The sister and brother raced over to their friends.

"So?" Gaby asked expectantly.

"Done." Jamal smiled. "We're just going to stick it into number one sixty-three's locker so he finds it in the morning. You're sure you want to go through with this, Alex?" he asked his friend.

"Absolutely," Alex whispered as his father passed by.

"Hi, kids," Mr. Fernandez called.

"Okay then, it's all systems go!" Lenni said. "See you guys in school tomorrow."

"Wait," Gaby called. "Let's see the message."

Lenni took the folded light-blue paper from her pocket and opened it for Alex and Gaby.

"Looks like official THABTO stuff to me," Gaby said. "Awesome work, you guys!"

Jamal and Lenni smiled at each other. "Teamwork, right? Let's just hope the rest of this case goes as well as this message did," Lenni said. She grabbed Jamal's arm. "Let's go or the building will be closed. Then we'll never get to the locker." They headed into the street.

"We can't run, because we don't want to call attention to ourselves, but let's walk sort of fast," Jamal said. "I want this part over with already."

"I'm with you," Lenni said as they quickened their pace to a brisk walk.

They reached the schoolyard. Kids were playing stickball and basketball. Backpacks were thrown on the ground. They walked into the building and straight to locker number 163.

"You be the lookout," Lenni said. "I'll stick it in the locker."

Jamal nodded and peeked around the corner.

"All clear," he whispered. Lenni pushed the note through the slit in the locker and walked quickly away.

"Okay," she said, walking up to Jamal. They walked briskly down the hall.

"It has been a long day," Jamal said as they walked out the door. "I'm ready to go home!"

They passed the park. Jamal looked in and remembered the weird dancers he had seen. He hoped they were about to find out the truth of what he had seen that night. And he hoped they weren't getting in too deep.

CHAPTER 13

A full moon cast huge shadows of old ships' smoke-stacks and masts across the silent Navy Yard.

Jamal, Lenni, and Gaby peered around nervously, standing by a railing overlooking the yard. Gaby gasped, clinging to Lenni, as a huge rat scampered down a stairway. The stairs led to an old warehouse next to the water, where big, leaky ships floated, waiting to be repaired.

Suddenly a THABTO walked quickly past the kids, not noticing them hiding in the shadows.

"Alex!" Gaby hissed when she spotted the THABTO.

"Let's go!" Alex ordered. The kids followed him, running to the entrance of the Navy Yard Building. Gaby ran to a window and peeked inside. The shadowy outlines of machinery looked like huge metal monsters. She ran back to the other kids.

"This place give me the creeps," she said.

"You want to go home?" Alex asked sharply.

Gaby gulped and shook her head.

"Then keep quiet!" Alex said. He looked around nervously for a sign of the other THABTOs.

"Okay," Gaby said. "But this is scaring me more than I thought."

"Chill out, it'll be fine," Alex said, his own heart pounding so loudly he was sure his friends could hear it.

Alex felt Jamal tug at his arm. "Over there!" Jamal whispered, pointing to two THABTOs greeting each other at the other end of the Navy Yard. Both wore double-faced masks and army belts and carried flashlights. One THABTO banged his flashlight on a trashcan lid as the pair walked backward toward each other.

"These guys are really weird!" Lenni whispered.

The kids crouched in the dark at the side of the building and watched the THABTO greeting ceremony.

"Double welcome," one THABTO said.

"Double welcome," replied the second. A third THABTO suddenly appeared out of the darkness. The first one banged the trashcan lid again and the third THABTO walked backward toward the waiting pair.

"Double welcome," he said.

"Double welcome to you, too," they replied.

Hiding in the shadows, the kids watched the THABTOs, who seemed to be impatiently waiting for the number four man.

"It looks like they're starting," Lenni said.

Suddenly Alex felt the panic rise into his throat. "What if locker one sixty-three shows up?" he asked.

"Sshh," Jamal said. "They're saying something."

"Where's our double-jointed brother?" the first THABTO asked.

"We can't start without him," the second said.

"He wasn't at the meeting place," the third THABTO said.

"Awwrrrright!" Lenni whispered. "Our note worked! You're on if you want to be, Alex."

"Listen, Alex," Jamal said seriously. "Are you sure you want to do this?"

"You don't have to if you don't want to, you know," Gaby said. "Jamal's tape recorder might be able to get everything down from where we are."

"But in case it doesn't, I need to be close enough to hear everything," Alex said, swallowing hard. "No, I'm going. Besides, you already sent that message to the fourth THABTO. And if I don't show up, there might not be a ceremony and then we'll have nothing."

He took a deep breath, put on his double-faced mask, and gripped his flashlight.

"Good luck, Alex," Gaby whispered.

"Thanks," he said. He walked to the end of the Navy Yard Building toward the THABTO ceremony.

"I hope this works," Jamal said, as he held up his miniature tape recorder.

The team members held their breaths. All eyes were on Alex as he got closer to the three THABTOs. His chest pounded and he breathed heavily. He heard the first THABTO greet him.

"Well, finally. Double welcome, THABTO," he said.

"Double welcome, THABTOs," Alex replied.

"Let the ceremony begin," the first one said. The second and third THABTOs took their positions facing the one who had called for the ceremony to begin. Alex did the same. They each held their flashlights under their masked faces.

In the shadows of the Navy Yard Building, Jamal, Lenni, and Gaby watched and waited nervously. The ceremony continued with the head THABTO leading an off-key chant that sounded like "With our quarters by our sides."

The other two THABTOs began repeating each line after the leader. Alex fell in quickly with the rest.

"With our quarters by our sides," Alex and the two THABTOs repeated.

"We'll do a Double Defenders ride," the leader sang.

"Then the tournament is ours," he chanted. "All will bow down to our powers, and know the THABTOs are next to none. Two heads are better than one."

The song erupted into a yelling, hooting scene of four wild THABTOs acting out Double Defenders moves.

Jamal, Lenni, and Gaby watched in disbelief.

"Oooooo, scary," Lenni whispered.

The singing and wild dancing stopped suddenly.

"And now," the leader said, "we will each sign in under our chosen name."

Alex gulped under his mask.

"Which name is Alex's?" Gaby whispered as they stared in horror.

"I don't know," Jamal said nervously.

"I don't think Alex knows either," Lenni said. "This could become a major disaster."

The leader pulled out a scroll, opened it, and signed his name with a flourish: *Mighty Masher.*

The next THABTO signed his with a large *Rocket Ripper.*

Then it was Alex's turn. Reluctantly he stepped up to the scroll. He knew he had two choices: Great Gripper or Kool Kicker.

"Boy, I hope he makes the right guess," Lenni whispered to Gaby.

With a flourish, Alex signed *Great Gripper* on the scroll.

The three THABTOs stared at him in silence.

"Hey," came the voice of a girl from behind the double-faced mask. "I'm Great Gripper!"

Alex froze. He looked nervously back and forth at the three genuine THABTOs.

"Who are you?" Mighty Masher shouted at Alex.

"We've been double-crossed!" Great Gripper shrieked.

Alex dropped his flashlight and ran. He sprinted toward the front of the Navy Yard Building, where Gaby, Jamal, and Lenni waited. "I'll catch you guys later . . . ," he called to the THABTOs, who were hot on his trail.

"Run! Run!" Alex called to his friends as he approached their hiding place. Jamal grabbed the tape recorder and shoved it inside his jacket.

Alex slowed down long enough to grab Gaby's hand. They raced inside the Navy Yard Building, followed by Rocket Ripper. They darted behind some huge machinery and stood still, barely breathing. Rocket Ripper stopped and looked around.

Lenni and Jamal took off in the other direction, into the moonlit night.

Alex and Gaby waited, frozen behind the machinery, their hearts still pounding. After a little while, Alex pulled off his double-faced mask and peeked around the machinery. He watched as Rocket Ripper looked under and around machinery, searching for them.

Alex and Gaby crouched low to the ground and silently slid halfway under a truck. Rocket Ripper walked deeper and deeper into the huge building.

When Alex and Gaby could no longer hear Rocket Ripper's footsteps, they slid out from under the truck and crept to the sign marked EXIT. Without making a sound, they opened the door and ran outside.

They scanned the empty yard for the other two THABTOs. Not only were there no THABTOs, but they saw no sign of Jamal and Lenni either.

"That was close," Gaby whispered.

Alex sighed. "I hope Jamal and Lenni made it all right. I really blew this one."

"It wasn't your fault," Gaby said.

"Let's just get out of here," Alex said. "We'll go to Lenni's loft where we said we'd meet."

* * *

Jamal and Lenni were having trouble shaking Mighty Masher and Great Gripper. They ran through the huge Navy Yard, but couldn't lose the two pursuing THABTOs. At last, Jamal pointed to an alley that looked as if it led out of the yard. With a final surge of energy Jamal and Lenni headed down it . . . and ran straight into a fence. It was too high for either of them to scale by themselves.

"I don't believe this!" Jamal whispered. "We're trapped."

They turned from the fence just in time to see the two THABTOs, still wearing their double-faced masks, coming toward them.

"Uh-oh." Lenni gulped.

"Do what I tell you," Jamal ordered, putting down the tape recorder and lacing his hands together to form a step. "Put your foot here!"

"What?" Lenni looked at him.

"Hurry up!" Jamal said as the THABTOs got closer.

With a boost from Jamal, Lenni scaled the wall.

"Give me the tape player," she told Jamal before she jumped down on the other side.

Jamal handed her the tape player. "I'll meet you back at your place," he called as she jumped to the ground and ran.

If I get out of this alive, he thought.

Jamal turned, his back against the fence. He stood face-to-face with the two THABTOs.

"Mr. Jenkins," Mighty Masher boomed angrily. "This is the second time you've gotten all mixed up in our business."

"Wasn't that warning last week clear enough for you?" Great Gripper asked.

"You know, man, you're looking to get permanently messed up if you keep minding our business!" Mighty Masher shouted.

The masked THABTOs lunged toward Jamal, ready to beat him up. But before they knew what had happened, Jamal grabbed their masks and pulled them up so that their eyes were covered.

"Hey," Mighty Masher cried, "what the . . ."

The pair flailed around blindly and fumbled with their masks. Jamal pushed through them, raced back down the alley, and ran up the steps to the street.

CHAPTER 14

"Stop pacing," Alex said to Lenni and Gaby. They were assembled in Lenni's loft, waiting for some word from Jamal.

"Jamal's a dynamite dude. He'll take care of himself. Trust me," Alex said.

The girls looked at Alex and rolled their eyes. "What if they beat him up?" Gaby said.

"What if he's hurt and needs help? Maybe we should go back to that alley and see if he's there," Lenni added, her eyes filling with tears.

Alex sighed. He felt responsible for the whole mess.

The three jumped when they heard a knock on the door.

"Who is it?" Lenni called.

"It's Jamal," came a familiar voice from the hallway.

Lenni opened the door and Jamal rushed in, still breathing heavily. Without thinking, Lenni hugged him.

"Are you okay?" she asked.

"Yeah," said Jamal, hugging her back. Alex and Gaby gathered around Jamal.

"I'm sure glad you're still in one piece," Lenni said. "Those THABTOs were out for revenge!"

"That makes two of us glad I'm out of there," Jamal said, looking at Lenni.

"So, how'd you get away?" Alex asked.

Jamal shook his head. "Man, like a running back punching through the line. I showed them a new way to wear those fancy masks they have!"

"All right!" Alex gave him a high five.

"Did they follow you?" Lenni asked, suddenly frightened.

"I don't think so," Jamal said.

Lenni went to the window and pulled up the shade, but she didn't see anyone.

"One thing I can tell you," Jamal said. "Those THABTOs are pretty bugged out."

"Sorry about picking the wrong name, Jamal," Alex said.

"It's all right, I guess," Jamal teased. "You couldn't be cool for anything!"

Jamal, Gaby, and Lenni laughed.

Alex swallowed and tried to change the subject. "Well, at least we got that chant down on tape," he said.

"Did you listen to it yet?" Jamal asked.

"I just finished writing it down," Gaby said, handing the paper to Jamal.

"Great," Jamal said. "Let's see if we can find anything more that might connect the THABTOs to the backpack thieves."

The team gathered around the paper. Suddenly the letters glowed brightly.

"Ghostwriter!" Gaby cried.

"He's reading along!" Alex said as they watched the letters on the page glow:

WITH OUR QUARTERS BY OUR SIDE,
WE'LL DO A DOUBLE DEFENDERS RIDE.
THEN THE TOURNAMENT WILL BE OURS.
ALL WILL BOW DOWN TO OUR POWERS
AND KNOW THE THABTOS ARE NEXT TO NONE.
TWO HEADS ARE BETTER THAN ONE!

The kids went over every word of the THABTO chant. Lenni pointed out that they used *quarters* and were confident they'd win the tournament.

"Hey, they must be talking about that Double Defenders tournament," Jamal said. "Remember, Alex? We saw a sign about it at the arcade."

Alex flashed back to the day he met Jamal at the video arcade and they watched four kids—the THABTOs—furiously playing Double Defenders. He remembered seeing the sign on the wall announcing the tournament.

"Yeah!" Alex said, jumping up. "And it's at the arcade, tomorrow, twelve noon!"

"So we know they'll be there," Lenni said, pointing to the paper.

"It takes a lot of money to practice those video games if you're determined to win," Jamal said.

"Which means lots and lots of quarters," Gaby said with disgust. "That's why they stole the money from me and the other kids. To play Double Defenders!"

"Those THABTOs are thieves, all right," Jamal said angrily.

Gaby shook her head in agreement. "And now we know why."

"We got 'em!" Alex cheered. "I can't wait until tomorrow!"

The words on the last line of the chant started glowing as the kids gathered around.

"Ghostwriter!" Jamal cried. "Look, he's highlighted the first letter of each word in the last line. He's sending us a message."

"'Two heads are better than one!'" Lenni read. "Why is he lighting up the first letter of every word?"

Alex shook his head. "I don't know."

"Wait," Jamal said excitedly. "Look. *T, H, A, B, T, O.*"

Alex jumped from his seat. "It spells THABTO!"

"Right," Lenni said. "Two heads are better than one!"

"Two heads!" Alex laughed, picking up his two-headed mask. "Like their two-headed masks. Boy, these guys are really hung up on the Double Defenders game."

"Hung up is one thing," Jamal said. "But it's like the

114

game is real to them or something. These guys should get a grip."

"What they should get is their heads handed to them on a platter," Lenni said angrily. "Stealing money just so they could practice—"

"Stealing *my* money," Gaby interrupted. "I ought to make them give it back!"

Jamal nodded in agreement. "They ought to give it back to all the kids. I don't care how bugged out these THABTOs are, we've got to be at the tournament tomorrow."

"But why would they even show up at the tournament after what happened tonight?" Lenni asked.

"'Cause Double Defenders is practically their life, that's why." Alex smirked.

"You're right," Jamal said. "And we're going to step right into it. Showdown at twelve o'clock tomorrow!"

"Right!" they cheered, giving each other the Ghostwriter handshake.

"We better get going," Jamal said. "My folks are going to send out the FBI if I don't get home pretty soon."

"Us, too," Gaby said, grabbing Alex's arm.

"See you, guys," Lenni said. "How about if we meet outside the arcade about a quarter to twelve?"

"Got quarters on the brain?" Gaby said.

"After the night we had," Lenni said, "I think I do."

CHAPTER 15

Jamal, Lenni, Gaby, and Alex gathered in front of the noisy arcade at a quarter to twelve. They watched crowds of kids file in for the Double Defenders tournament.

"I can't believe how many of these kids can get so into this stuff," Gaby said. "And then to steal money to be able to play games."

"Unfortunately, it's the same thing thugs of all ages do," Lenni said. "Steal from people and use it for their own gain."

"I don't think all the kids who play games do that," Jamal said. "You just find some creeps in every group."

116

"Well, these THABTOs sure are creeps," Gaby said.

They stood around outside talking for a while. Gaby peeked into the arcade.

"I think the first round is already ended," she reported.

Inside the arcade, the THABTOs were jumping and shouting wildly as they played their second round in the tournament.

The opposing team members glanced dejectedly at the scoreboard, which showed the THABTOs with a big lead in the first round.

The sign showed:

TEAM	FIRST ROUND
THABTOS	56,810
DRAGONS	45,900
MARVELS	37,218
PROTECTORS	25,735

The noisy second round continued with the THABTOs shrieking orders to one another.

"Look out, Rocket! Near your other head!" screamed Great Gripper, as she jumped up and down.

Electricity filled the air as the sounds of the video game mingled with the screamed orders from team members.

No one noticed Jamal walking boldly into the arcade, carrying his tape recorder. Jamal faced the tournament players. Lenni, Alex, and Gaby followed and stood beside Jamal.

Then, one by one, the kids whose backpacks had been

stolen filed in and stood behind the team. They looked angry and determined.

The THABTOs and other players didn't see the mob of kids behind them.

Jamal turned to one little girl standing in the group who had appeared in Tina's video about the backpack thefts.

"Gaby said you saw the face of your robber. And that you heard somebody call him Rocket Ripper," Jamal said.

The girl nodded. "Uh-huh."

Jamal turned back to the THABTOs and shouted, "Run, Rocket Ripper, run!"

Rocket Ripper whipped around, shocked to see the angry, glaring kids.

"That's him," the little girl said, pointing to Rocket Ripper. "He's the one who stole my backpack!"

The other three THABTOs spun around, their eyes wide with surprise.

"What are you talking about?" Rocket Ripper asked in a panicky voice. "What backpack?"

"Shoot!" Kool Kicker shouted. "Game's over!"

"Look," Mighty Masher said in a nasty tone. "We've got an important tournament. And you guys are trying to ruin it for us." He turned his back on them and moved to the game machine. "Now if you don't mind . . ."

Jamal held up a THABTO button he had taken from his pocket. "Which one of you guys lost this great-looking button?" he asked. "I know it couldn't be Dan, or could it?"

The THABTOs looked at each other.

"So, two heads *are* better than one. Right, THABTOs?" Alex said, smirking.

Now the THABTOs looked nervously from one to the other.

Gaby took a handful of coded messages on light-blue paper from her pocket and held them up for all to see.

"And what about all these coded messages you left in our backpacks?" she asked, as the THABTOs' faces started to lose color. "Let me decode it for you," she said, without reading: "'Neat and clean I got away. Hey hey.'"

The THABTOs didn't move but looked less and less sure of themselves as the other tournament players started a buzz of conversation around them.

"Good thing we cracked your code, guys," Lenni said. "Otherwise we couldn't have sent your Kool Kicker a coded message so that he couldn't make it to your final ceremony."

"Speaking of which," Jamal said, smiling as he held up his tape recorder. He pressed the Play button and turned up the volume so that no one could miss the voices of the THABTOs, including Alex, chanting their ritual the night before in the Navy Yard.

As the chant played loudly, the THABTOs grew panicky. Jamal, Lenni, Gaby, and Alex waited for them to make a move. When the chant ended, Jamal shut off the recorder. The arcade was strangely silent, but a loud tension filled the air.

"What's the matter, guys?" Jamal said. "Can't make a move without your stupid masks on?"

Alex pulled his double-faced mask from behind his back

and held it up. There were gasps of surprise from the THABTOs, the kids behind Jamal, and the other tournament players.

"We want our money back, THABTOs!" Gaby shouted.

"Yeah!" the kids who had lost backpacks yelled in agreement. "Where is it?"

The THABTOs looked at each other and then suddenly darted among the packed crowds of players and onlookers, trying to get away.

Several kids pounced on them, trying to stop them. They shoved and kicked their way through the crowd, pushing people onto the floor until they reached an exit sign at the back. They raced out the door, leaving a trail of bumps and bruises behind them.

"Let them go," Jamal said over the angry shouts of the crowd.

Moments later, the four thugs reappeared in the doorway, pushed back into the arcade by two uniformed police officers.

A cheer rose in the arcade as the kids saw the police officers.

"Okay, keep it down in here," one police officer said. "We received information from these young detectives"— he pointed to Jamal, Lenni, Alex, and Gaby—"about the problems you kids have been having with backpack thefts. This information seems to make you kids suspects," he said, pointing to the THABTOs.

"Yeah, they're the ones," a girl shouted. "I saw them."

"Lock them up," another boy yelled.

"Before we do any locking up, let's hear what these kids have to say for themselves," the officer said, turning to the fidgeting THABTOs.

After a moment of hesitation, Mighty Masher spoke. "We just needed the money for practice, for the game. We didn't take anything else from the backpacks, we didn't really hurt anyone. We're Double Defenders players. Good players. The best!"

"No," Alex shouted back. "You're not Double Defenders *anything*. You're not superheroes. You're super-cowards!"

"All right," one officer said to the four THABTOs. "Let's go. I think it's time we called your parents."

The THABTOs walked out with the policemen, their heads bowed.

"And don't worry, kids," the other officer said as they pushed through the crowd. "I'm sure these THABTOs will be paying your money back real soon!"

The kids cheered. Some went up to shake hands with Jamal, Alex, Gaby, and Lenni.

"Man, what a great feeling!" Jamal said.

"We did it!" Gaby shouted.

"Blasted 'em right out of the water!" Alex said, laughing.

"And they won't be playing Double Defenders again anytime soon," Gaby said.

"Or stealing again ever, I hope," Lenni added.

The four stood looking around the arcade. The big moment was over and the team felt let down after all the drama and excitement. The crowds thinned out as the players went back to the competition and other kids left.

"You know, it was kind of tense for a moment there, wasn't it?" Jamal said.

"Yes," Gaby agreed.

"But," Alex pointed out, "we had our backup."

"Right," Jamal said.

They stood around unsure of what to say or do next.

"So . . . that's it, huh?" Gaby asked.

"I guess so," Alex said. "Case closed."

"It feels kind of weird after all the excitement, doesn't it?" Gaby said. "But I guess it's over. I have to say, Alex," she said to her brother, "this detective stuff was more fun than I ever imagined."

"It was fun to be together, wasn't it?" Jamal said, reluctant to see the group go their separate ways. He thought about how Ghostwriter had brought them together and helped them solve the mystery. Now they were saying good-bye and Jamal was somehow sorry that it was all coming to an end.

"I've got to get home now that we've finished our work," Lenni said.

"We do, too," Alex said. "We've got work to do in the store."

Jamal stood silently.

"You coming, Jamal?" Lenni asked as they turned to leave.

"No . . . that's all right. You guys go ahead," Jamal said, as Lenni, Alex, and Gaby headed out.

"Bye, Jamal," they called.

"See you," he said, gripping his tape recorder and looking around the arcade.

After a few minutes he sighed and walked out the door.

"Well, I guess that's it," he said to himself. "It's over."

CHAPTER 16

The Brooklyn streets were busy with shoppers and families as Jamal trudged home. He felt himself nudged and pushed as the crowds hurried along, but didn't really care.

"Where've you been?" Grandma CeCe called from the kitchen when Jamal got to his house. "I've been worried!"

"Come on, I'm a big boy now. Quit your worrying!"

"Okay," she said. "Sit down for some of my scrumptious seafood salad."

"I'm not really hungry," Jamal said.

"What is this, the Brooklyn Diner?" she asked. "Okay, I'll leave a sandwich for you in the fridge because I've got to do some shopping."

"Thanks, Grandma," Jamal said, picking up his tape player and going to his room.

Jamal closed the door and put the tape player in his drawer. He spotted the old baseball cap he'd found in the basement with his father when they were looking for the trunk for Danitra to take to college. That seemed like such a long time ago. So much had happened since then.

He pushed it on backward over his close-cut hair, found his favorite baseball and glove, and plopped onto his bed, tossing and catching the ball.

Suddenly he noticed the papers on the bulletin board near his desk. Glowing yellow letters flashed wildly around.

HELLO, JAMAL, the message from Ghostwriter said.

Jamal smiled. He put down his ball and glove and grabbed a pen and a piece of paper that already had some writing on it.

"Are you with Lenni, Alex, and Gaby, too?" Jamal read his message to Ghostwriter.

Ghostwriter pulled letters from the words to respond.

I AM WITH YOU ALL, Ghostwriter's message read.

Jamal smiled. He was glad Ghostwriter had come into his life. It was weird and he couldn't explain it, but it felt good. He looked at the pen in his hand and suddenly jumped up. He went to his closet and took down an old shoe box on which he'd written SECRET MONEY. He counted the money. Four dollars and some change.

"That should do it," he said under his breath, cramming the money into his pocket. Jamal put on his jacket and raced out of his room, down the stairs, and out of the house. He walked briskly, dodging his way through the crowds. He turned the corner, walked several blocks, and entered The Party Animal store.

He waved to Calvin, Alex's obnoxious classmate, who stood behind the counter with his pet parrot, Attila, and his mother, Mrs. Ferguson. Jamal winced as he heard Mrs. Ferguson telling a customer about her wonderful Calvin.

". . . and he's a very good athlete, too . . . probably the best soccer player in the whole school . . . plays the piano . . . studies everything. He's just so talented . . ."

Jamal walked around the store and found what he was looking for. He placed four pieces of colored string and four colored pens on the counter.

"I'd like to get these, please," he said to Mrs. Ferguson.

"Calvin will take care of you," she said, running off at the mouth again. "I'm making his favorite dinner. Tuna fish, mashed potatoes, peas mashed all together, just the way he—"

"Ma!" Calvin silenced her. She gave him a big, sloppy kiss on the cheek, waved to Attila, and headed out the door.

Calvin quickly pulled himself together.

"What's up, homey?" he said to Jamal.

"Would you mind just ringing my stuff up, please," Jamal replied.

Calvin went to the register to tally the items. "Everyone's just buzzing about your THABTO capture. How did you and Alex and Lenni suddenly get so clever?" he asked.

Jamal handed Calvin the money.

"That's for us to know and you to find out," he said, smiling slyly.

Calvin sneered as he handed Jamal his package. "Is that a challenge?"

"Just give me my stuff, man!"

"You're up to something," Calvin said. "But don't try to hide it from me. I'll find out one way or another."

"Sure," Jamal said.

"*Aarrk!*" Attila shrieked. "You're brilliant, Calvin."

Jamal grabbed his bag and left the store. He had work to do.

CHAPTER 17

The house was empty when Jamal got home. "Now I'm hungry," he said to no one in particular as he headed for the refrigerator and found the sandwich Grandma CeCe had left.

He poured a glass of milk and sat at the kitchen table, looking at his purchases from The Party Animal.

Jamal devoured the sandwich. He picked up the pens and string and headed for his room.

Sitting on his bed, he attached a string to the end of each pen. He picked up the last pen, inspected it, and said out loud, "Well, Ghostwriter, I hope this works."

He took a deep breath and reached for a piece of paper. Using the new pen, he wrote, "Rally J."

Ghostwriter's sparkling glow moved quickly back and forth over the message. Jamal sat back and looked at what he'd just written.

"Now we wait and see," he said, and he picked up a comic and started to read.

After helping their father with afternoon chores in the bodega, Gaby went to the bedroom to read. Alex stayed in the store to handle the register.

Lying on her bed, Gaby skimmed through her favorite trivia book, still excited about the THABTO capture. Suddenly she noticed a change on her book cover.

The message glowed in blue letters: RALLY J.

"'Rally J?'" she said out loud, then burst into a huge grin. "All right!"

Gaby ran out to the bodega and pulled Alex aside. She whispered to him about the book and the message.

"Really? Wow!" he said. "Let me see if Papa will let us go to Jamal's house."

Mr. Fernandez sat on a stool at the counter, looking over the receipts.

"Papa?" Alex said. "If you don't need me here anymore could Gaby and I go to Jamal's house?"

"We won't be long, Papa," Gaby piped up. "Just a short meeting."

Mr. Fernandez nodded. "All right. You kids did a good thing getting those thugs who were stealing money, so you can have some extra time off. Just don't be late for dinner."

"Thank you, Papa," they said, as they bolted out the door.

Lenni sat alone in her loft, reading a comic book and munching cookies. Her father was playing at an afternoon gig and wouldn't be home for a while. She closed the comic and rubbed her eyes. Then she spotted the cover with the glowing blue message: RALLY J.

"Hey," she said, smiling. "I guess it works."

She put down her comic, scribbled a note to her father, grabbed a sweater, and left the loft, making sure to double-lock after she closed the door. Sprinting down the stairs, she ran into the street, where she bumped head-on into Alex and Gaby.

The trio looked at each other and broke into big grins. "You, too?" Lenni said. The brother and sister nodded.

Minutes later, they ran up the stairs to Jamal's house and rang the bell. Grandma CeCe opened the door.

"Well, hello!" she said warmly. "You're all out of breath! Come in. Jamal's up in his room. Can I get you a snack or something?"

"No thank you," they said.

"We'll just go on up," Lenni said, anxiously leading the way.

"Nice kids," Grandma CeCe said as she walked back into the kitchen. "But they never eat!"

Jamal jumped when he heard the knock at his door and pulled it open as Lenni, Alex, and Gaby rushed in.

"What's up, man? Another case?" Alex asked expectantly.

"Another little kid being picked on by big kids?" Gaby asked before Jamal could reply.

"Somebody in trouble?" Lenni asked.

"Well," Jamal said, "not exactly."

"Well, then, what is it?" Gaby pressed, her eyes lighting up with excitement. "A surprise?"

Jamal smiled. "More like an idea."

"What do you mean?" Lenni asked, looking confused.

"Well, I was thinking about all the awesome times we've had since we met Ghostwriter, and I mean, if the THABTOs were a team, why can't *we* be a team?"

"Yeah," Alex said. "We'll be a team of young detectives, we'll wear sunglasses and we'll have miniature video cameras in our boots . . ."

Jamal laughed. "Well, my idea wasn't quite so high-tech, but I think you'll like it."

He took out the pens with the colored string attached.

"What's this?" Lenni asked.

Jamal put the string with the pen around his neck to demonstrate and then put one on each team member.

"They're our official Ghostwriter pens," he said.

"That's great!" Gaby said.

Lenni looked at the pen and smiled. "Way cool!"

"We can write to Ghostwriter anytime, anyplace," Jamal explained.

"Why don't we tell him what's going on?" Alex suggested. "Let's write to him now. Besides, he's on the team, too."

Alex took a piece of paper and unwrapped his Ghostwriter pen.

"Yeah," Gaby agreed. "He's the whole reason *for* the team. I mean, we wouldn't *be* a team without Ghostwriter!"

The four kids stopped for a moment and looked at each other.

"That's right," Alex said.

Lenni turned to Jamal. "Do you remember when we first met Ghostwriter? He was so sad and lonely, he almost went away!"

"Yes, I know," Jamal said. "He didn't even know who he was! But we wrote to him and we brought him back."

"And now we know a lot of things about him," Lenni pointed out.

"Tell me," Alex said to Lenni. "I'll write them down."

"Okay," Lenni said. "He cares about children . . ."

"Got it!" Alex said, still writing. "He also likes to help solve mysteries."

"Let me see what you've got," Lenni said, as she took the paper from Alex. He had written:

Things we know about Ghostwriter:
　　—You care about children.
　　—You like mysteries.

"Now I'll write," Lenni said, as she added: "You fight for what's right."

Gaby took the paper. "You thirst for knowledge," she added.

"And he's our friend," Jamal pointed out. "And he has feelings he can't even put into words."

Jamal went to the paper and added to the list: "You are a friend."

Lenni looked over the list and chuckled. "You know what's so funny?"

"What?" Jamal asked.

"These are the things we care about, too!"

"And that's what makes us a team!"

"One for all and all for one," Alex joined in. "Besides, we have our own handshake!"

"And the Rally call," Jamal pointed out.

"We should get T-shirts!" Gaby said.

"And songs!" Lenni added.

"Hey, you know what?" Alex said. "Maybe if we keep on writing down everything we know about Ghostwriter, then someday we can help him solve the *big* mystery about who he is!"

The kids looked at each other and sighed.

"That would be awesome!" Lenni said. "Okay, we need a name."

"I know what we should call ourselves," Jamal said. "The Ghostwriter Team."

"Yes! That's it! I like it!" they all said at once.

"Hey, I've got it," Jamal said. He bolted for his closet and fished out a tattered old leather book. He held it out to the team.

"What do you think?" he asked.

The others looked at him as if he were crazy.

"What is it?" Gaby asked.

"It's a notebook!" Jamal said. "I found it in the basement. Grandma says that ghosts live in memories and good old things. I say we keep everything we find out about Ghostwriter in here."

"Great idea," Gaby said. "Let's start with these notes that we just wrote."

Jamal opened the dusty notebook. A hush fell over the room as Alex took the page of notes and put it inside.

"This is so cool!" Lenni said.

"The Official Ghostwriter Team Book," Jamal said.

"But wait . . . ," Gaby said. "We forgot the most important thing."

"What?" Lenni, Alex, and Jamal all asked at the same time.

Gaby took a piece of paper and wrote:

GHOSTWRITER TEAM
Do you like that name?

Just as Gaby finished writing, Ghostwriter's glow flew onto the paper and lifted the words up into the air.

I LIKE GHOSTWRITER TEAM, he wrote.

"I think you just got your answer," Lenni beamed.

"All right!" Jamal said, giving Alex a high five.

The words swirled around the kids. As Jamal held the book in the air, the words zoomed inside. Jamal closed the cover as if to catch them.

"What do you think is happening?" Lenni asked.

The others shrugged, gathering around Jamal. He waited a moment and then opened the book. Magically, a new page had appeared in the book that said OUR GHOSTWRITER TEAM MYSTERY BOOK.

"Yes!" Gaby cheered. "Let's hear it for Ghostwriter!"

"And teamwork," Lenni added.

"And mysteries." Alex beamed.

Jamal put down the book. "And lots and lots of adventures," he said, as he started them off with the Ghostwriter handshake.

"Hands in the center and go with me," Alex said.

Alex put his hand in the center. Jamal, Lenni, and Gaby followed his lead.

"Follow me on the count of three!" Alex said. "One, two, three!"

The team crossed hands and joined Alex as he raised them into the air, shouting: *"Gghooooosstttttwriter!"*

From the
Hit TV Show

Ghost writer

Created by CTW

BECOME AN OFFICIAL
GHOSTWRITER READERS CLUB MEMBER!

You'll receive the following GHOSTWRITER Readers Club Materials:
Official Membership Card • The Scoop on GHOSTWRITER •
GHOSTWRITER Magazine
All members registered by December 31st will have a chance to win
a FREE COMPUTER and other exciting prizes!

OFFICIAL ENTRY FORM

Mail your completed entry to: Bantam Doubleday Dell BFYR,
GW Club, 1540 Broadway, New York, NY 10036

Name

Address

City   **State**   **Zip**

Date of birth   **Phone**

Club Sweepstakes Official Rules
1. No purchase necessary. Enter by completing and returning the Entry Coupon. All entries must be received by Bantam
   Doubleday Dell no later than December 31, 1993. No mechanically reproduced entries allowed. By entering the
   sweepstakes, each entrant agrees to be bound by these rules and the decision of the judges which shall be final and binding.
   Limit: one entry per person.
2. The prizes are as follows: Grand Prize: One computer with monitor (approximate retail value of Grand Prize $3,000), First
   Prizes: Ten GHOSTWRITER libraries (approximate retail value of each First Prize: $25), Second Prizes: Five GHOSTWRITER
   backpacks (approximate retail value of each Second Prize: $25), and Third Prizes: Ten GHOSTWRITER T-Shirts (approximate
   retail value of each Third Prize: $10). Winners will be chosen in a random drawing on or about January 10, 1994, from
   among all completed Entry Coupons received and will be notified by mail. Odds of winning depend on the number of
   entries received. No substitution or transfer of the prize is allowed. All entries become property of BDD and will not be
   returned. Taxes, if any, are the sole responsibility of the winner. BDD reserves the right to substitute a prize of equal or
   greater value if any prize becomes unavailable.
3. This sweepstakes is open only to the residents of the U.S. and Canada, excluding the Province of Quebec, who are between
   the ages of 6 and 14 at the time of entry. The winner, if Canadian, will be required to answer correctly a time-limited
   arithmetical skill testing question in order to receive the prize. Employees of Bantam Doubleday Dell Publishing Group Inc.
   and its subsidiaries and affiliates and their immediate family members are not eligible. Void where prohibited or restricted
   by law. Grand and first prize winners will be required to execute and return within 14 days of notification an affidavit of
   eligibility and release to be signed by winner and winner's parent or legal guardian. In the event of noncompliance with
   this time period, an alternate winner will be chosen.
4. Entering the sweepstakes constitutes permission for use of the winner's name, likeness, and biographical data for publicity
   and promotional purposes on behalf of BDD, with no additional compensation. For the name of the winner, available after
   January 31, 1994, send a self-addressed envelope, entirely separate from your entry, to Bantam Doubleday Dell, BFYR
   Marketing Department, 1540 Broadway, New York, NY 10036.

From the Hit TV Show

Ghost writer

Created by CTW

GHOSTWRITER—READ IT! SOLVE IT! TELL A FRIEND! CHECK OUT THESE GHOSTWRITER BOOKS.